Highway to Hell

Zombie Chaos Book 2

by

D.L. Martone

For our parents,
who have long supported us,
even if they'll likely never read a zompoc

Chapter

1

"They may not seem like much one at a time, but in a group, all riled up and hungry... Man, you watch your ass." – Morgan Jones, *The Walking Dead* (2010)

"You gotta be fucking kidding me," I muttered, gripping the steering wheel with renewed frustration.

In my never-ending effort to flee the New Orleans

area, I'd hoped to follow Earhart Expressway to Clearview Parkway, which would've resulted in a brief trip to Airline Drive. But thanks to a pileup of abandoned cars, decaying bodies, and twitching zombies on the northbound exit, I'd been forced to head south on Clearview, the wrong goddamn direction from my intended target.

I'd just passed the multiplex theater where my wife, Clare, and I had spent countless enjoyable hours together (one of many places we'd have to forfeit in the brave new zombie world) when I'd encountered what seemed like my hundredth traffic jam. For some inexplicable reason, numerous idiotic motorists had tried to escape the undead city by taking the Huey P. Long Bridge across the Mississippi River, a route that appeared to be jam-packed with charred vehicles and roaming zombies. Since I had no intention of getting my fortified step van stuck at the top of that stupid-ass bridge and risk plummeting into Ol' Man River, I'd impulsively taken a shortcut, hoping to find an easy way to turn around and retrace my route north.

As I'd long suspected, though, *hope* was a fucking four-letter word.

To untangle myself from the traffic jam, I'd careened the wrong way down Jefferson Highway and pulled into a familiar Walmart parking lot. I'd visited that particular store many times during the decade Clare and I had called New Orleans home. Oddly enough, it was one of the few places that stocked my favorite locally made fishing lure, which had ensured me and my wife plenty of success while casting for speckled trout in Lake Pontchartrain and the bayous near the Gulf of Mexico. Yet another Louisiana pastime I'd forever miss.

Goddamn zombie apocalypse.

Unfortunately, my plan had fallen to shit when I'd noticed the ridiculous number of zombies and automobiles blocking much of the parking lot. Perhaps it shouldn't have surprised me that, in the wake of an undead epidemic, many New Orleanians and local suburbanites had rushed to a Walmart in Harahan to stock up on supplies, only to find themselves overrun, bitten, and transformed into mindless carnivores. But due to the exhausting day I'd already had, my situational awareness wasn't as sharp as usual.

Afraid to get trapped by the ravenous horde, I'd immediately jerked the steering wheel to the left and made a rumbling beeline toward the alley that ran behind the store.

"Sorry, Azazel," I'd said, turning toward the cat carrier I'd secured in the passenger seat. "Daddy screwed up, but he's gonna get us outta this mess."

Having noted the carrier was empty, I'd recalled that, after successfully chasing some inconsiderate yuppie passengers out of my van with a tear gas canister, I'd released Azazel, my seven-year-old tabby, from her temporary prison. So, it was anyone's guess as to which nook or cranny she'd decided to curl up inside for a while.

Must be nice, kitty. Wish I had time for a fucking nap.

Just then, as I turned back to the windshield, still musing about Azazel's whereabouts (and wishing we could trade places for a bit), I suddenly found myself staring at a parked minivan, which inconveniently blocked my route about halfway down the rear alley. Cursing to myself, I slammed on my brakes to avoid a collision, but the next viable option eluded me.

A quick glance in my one still-functioning side-view mirror informed me I had unwanted company. Lots of it.

Apparently, one of the zombies in the parking lot (if not more) had noticed the careening meals-on-wheels that had ducked behind Walmart, and after that curious creature had shifted my way, many more had followed suit. A shitload of foul, undead monsters presently stumbled and trotted into the back alley, aimed directly for my van.

Awesome. What's next?

I knew reversing out of there would be impossible.

Given the narrow width of the rear access lane, I could never plow my way through such an enormous zombie horde. At most, I might be able to squish a few of the relentless creatures and carve out a twenty-foot-long path before getting my wheels stuck in the carnage and my van surrounded by the countless predators that remained.

Likewise, if I tried to plow through the minivan blockade, I'd risk getting hung up on the crushed metal and fiberglass – even with the steel bars across the front of my van. And then where would I be? Just as ensnared by the approaching zombies.

Shit, they're a hundred feet deep. Fuck. That's a lot of goddamn pus-sacks.

My only saving grace? The closest ones were still far enough away that I had a little time to deal with the situation. Maybe two minutes before the crowd would overwhelm my van, trapping me and my poor cat and ensuring we'd never see Clare again.

With no time to spare, I grabbed my trusty 12-gauge shotgun, which I'd wedged beneath the passenger seat. Then, after making certain the Mossberg was loaded, I climbed down from the van, slid the door shut (in case Azazel emerged from her nesting spot), and rapidly assessed the problem before me.

The vehicle blocking my path was parked at a perpendicular angle to the alley, its front grill pointed away from the building, as if the driver had been trying to turn the minivan around before his life had gone sideways. Due to the blood-drenched windows, I couldn't see the interior of the vehicle, but I assumed no one was alive inside. Of course, that didn't mean no one was moving.

In fact, while cautiously approaching the minivan, I observed a pair of hands pawing at one of the side windows. It was hard to say whether the sound of a moaning, hissing zombie horde or the prospect of fresh meat outside had roused the vehicle's occupants, but either way, the frenzied fingers managed to wipe away enough smeared blood to allow me a glimpse inside the minivan. Three figures jostled around inside: two in the front seats, one in the middle.

Quickly, I slid open the side door and hopped backward. A fat zombie, wearing an old-fashioned blue-and-yellow Walmart vest, tumbled from the minivan and onto the pavement. As he righted himself and stumbled toward me, I realized the zombie looked familiar. He had a round belly, shaggy hair, a scruffy beard, and tired half-moons under his eyes. Given his wrinkles and graying hair, I assumed he'd been in his sixties before transforming into the rotting, bloodstained creature he'd become, and at some point in his time as a zombie, he'd gained yet another disgusting attribute: part of a large human nose entangled in his beard.

"Well, that isn't yours," I quipped as I raised the Mossberg and shot him in the head.

Pumping another shell into the chamber, I watched him crumple to the ground. My focus drifted from the unsightly, goo-rimmed hole in his skull to the name tag on his uniform: *Davey*. No wonder he'd seemed so familiar: I'd often seen him at the front doors of Walmart, lazily greeting shoppers as they ventured into the store. Usually, he had a couple of old cohorts with him, two other Walmart greeters well past their prime. No doubt the pair of fidgeting zombies in the front seats of the minivan.

Before the zombie infection had spread to New Orleans, none of the three guys had ever seemed particularly pleased with their jobs (or with one another), and I'd always wondered how the disgruntled, bickering threesome had landed their greeting gigs, much less the same shifts. Some big-hearted manager must've taken pity on the downtrodden trio – and yet graciously refrained from subjecting other greeters to their bitter antics.

Sorry, boys. I'm all outta pity.

With a zombie horde breathing down my neck, I had no time to waste. I stepped over Davey's motionless feet, opened the driver's-side door, and watched as another zombie stumbled out, falling to his knees. Dressed in khaki pants, a white Oxford shirt, and a more stylish Walmart vest, the former greeter was much slimmer than the first one. He had a small, angular face, with dyed brown hair, perfectly coiffed.

Despite the decaying flesh and bloody streaks on his clothes, John (as his name tag read) was one of the tidiest zombies I'd yet seen. Well, except for the enormous chunk missing from his upper right arm. Given Davey's blood-spattered beard, I suspected he'd taken the chip out of John. I just wasn't sure if that had occurred before or after Davey had bitten off someone's sizable schnoz. John's nose, after all, was still intact.

The trim greeter had started pushing himself to his feet when I pulled the trigger. With an explosive whop, the slug deepened the part in his hair, carved a ridge from his forehead to the back of his skull, and sprayed blood, brain matter, and black zombie goo all over the minivan and nearby pavement. John rocked backward from the force of the slug, then crumpled at the knees and collapsed forward across Davey's thighs.

By the time I'd pumped the shotgun, the third zombie had crawled through the driver's-side door and emerged from the vehicle. Taller and skinnier than the other two, he only had a smattering of gray in his hair, but not surprisingly, he was missing much of his nose. No doubt, the rest of it was still entwined in his former greeting buddy's beard. As a result, the last of the unfortunate trio was the most disgusting, with rivulets of awful, foul-smelling black zombie goo dribbling from his shredded nasal cavity.

I glanced at his name tag. "Well, Shaun," I muttered, aiming the shotgun, "looks like the end of your fucking shift."

He responded by groaning and swatting at the barrel.

"Sorry, Chief. Should've gotten a real job." I retreated a couple of steps and pulled the trigger.

It no longer mattered that his pal had bitten off his nose; the shotgun blast pretty much removed the rest of his face, and he fell backward across the other two greeters.

More than likely, they'd sought refuge in the minivan after zombies had invaded their place of employment, but at least one of them must've been infected, resulting in the carnage I'd just witnessed.

Well, you lived together, and you died together. Who can ask for more than that?

Given the groans and hisses loudening behind me, I turned to check on the horde's progress.

"Fuck."

Some of the creatures were faster than I'd estimated. I didn't have much time.

Quickly, I stepped over the former Walmart greeters and peered around the sticky steering wheel. Though the key was in the ignition, the damn thing was still in the *on* position.

Figuring the battery was likely dead and the stupid minivan wouldn't start, I set the Mossberg down on the seat, jammed the shifter into neutral, cranked the wheel all the way to the right, and pushed the vehicle as close to the building as I could. When the right headlight smacked into the concrete wall, I shifted the minivan back into park, reclaimed the shotgun, and darted back to my own vehicle.

With the closest zombie only a few yards away, I yanked open my driver's-side door and found myself staring into the wide, green eyes of Azazel, who'd apparently jumped into my seat while I'd been busy dispatching the trio of zombified greeters.

"Jesus, kitty, you scared the shit outta me!"

Hastily, I slid the shotgun onto the floor, hopped into the van, slammed the door shut, and engaged the lock. Ignoring Azazel's customary harrumphs, I shoved her off my seat, turned the key in the ignition, and stepped on the gas pedal.

While I'd had no time to push the minivan flush against the building, I had straightened it enough for my immediate needs. So, after rolling over the tragic trio, my rumbling, fortified vehicle managed to squeeze past the minivan and continue down the alley.

Perfect timing, too, since I heard several loud thunks

as the nearest zombies hurled themselves at the rear and sides of my step van. From the odd scraping sounds I discerned amid the thumps and moans, I also suspected I was dragging something via my back bumper, but I had no desire to stop the vehicle and investigate the situation. I just hoped it wasn't one of the former Walmart greeters.

Not that it mattered. I had a much bigger problem on my hands: As I headed to the far side of the alley, hundreds of zombies poured around the corner of the building.

Hell, this group's even bigger than the one behind me!

Given my tendency toward bad luck, the sudden inundation of walking corpses shouldn't have shocked me. But, frankly, I'd hoped to avoid becoming part of an enormous zombie sandwich.

"Son of a fucking bitch," I grumbled. "Give me a goddamn break!"

No such thing, though: Both hordes were too dense for me to penetrate, even with my badass van.

I glanced at Azazel, who'd jumped on top of her carrier, not inside it (where I preferred her to be). "Sorry, girl. Looks like we gotta do something drastic."

As if translating *drastic* to *stupid*, she harrumphed once and wedged herself against the passenger seat.

Since I'd visited that Walmart many times before, I was intimately familiar with the layout. I knew, for example, that the automotive center sat alongside the building, between our current position and the zombie horde in front of us. So, to free us from our sticky situation, I intended to ram my way into one of the five available service bays.

Fortunately, my crazy-ass plan proved unnecessary. As I rolled down the alley, I noticed that the closest of the large, overhead garage doors was miraculously up.

My skeptical inner voice questioned the good fortune: Why was the door open? Had any zombies wandered inside because of it?

But I had no time ponder whether it was good or bad luck. I needed a temporary port in the storm – or just a viable route out of the alley.

Without overthinking it, I pulled the steering wheel hard to the right, slipped into the darkened bay, and stomped on the brakes. My back end cleared the opening just as my front bumper tapped an old, metallic blue Ford Focus that someone had left behind.

A hasty glance through my grimy windshield indicated three key factors in my future escape from Walmart. One, the five front-facing, overhead doors of the auto center were all closed, meaning I couldn't just step on the gas and shoot out the other side (*shit*). Two, I wasn't completely in the dark yet, as each of the doors featured a row of small windows that enabled dusty shafts of late-afternoon sunlight to illuminate parts of the shadowy space. And three, I'd likely have to use the compact car ahead of me as a makeshift battering ram.

Terrific. What can go wrong?

First, though, I had to keep the zombies outside from getting inside.

After pocketing my keys, I grabbed the shotgun, jumped to the ground, and slammed the door shut. Then I darted toward the wide-open entrance, wishing I could reach the overhead door and yank it closed. But alas, I wasn't twelve feet tall.

I glanced around the murky space, which still boasted the familiar scents of oil, sweat, and gasoline, but no glowing lights or other signs of working electricity. So, it probably didn't matter that I needed a key to operate the control box mounted beside the open doorway. It wouldn't function anyway.

Taking a chance that destroying said box would somehow release the overhead door, I aimed my Mossberg and pulled the trigger. Shards of the ravaged control panel flew everywhere, but naturally, the door didn't budge an inch.

Worse, the sound of the reverberating gunshot nearly

deafened me – and undoubtedly caused the converging zombie hordes to quicken their pace. In fact, I observed several eager creatures heading my way.

"Fucking door."

I scoped out the bay, looking for anything that could help me pull the door down, but the light was too spotty to see much – including obstacles in my path.

During my mad search, I knocked over several toolboxes, sending various sockets and wrenches skittering across the concrete floor. I accidentally toppled a few folding chairs as well. Some grease-stained uniform shirts slipped off the chairs, spilling their contents, which amounted to little more than cigarettes, lighters, and a few joints.

Good to know the mechanics had taken their jobs seriously.

Not that I've got anything against smoking a little weed, but really, guys? On the job?

What did it matter, though? The grease monkeys who'd once worked there were likely all dead.

I would be, too, if I didn't hurry. Gazing at the open bay door, I could see the zombies fast approaching from both sides.

Less than ten seconds, and the hordes would reach me. No time left to scavenge for tools. I'd just have to dive back into the van and wait out the undead storm. Experience had taught me, however, that zombies were a relentless lot – and unlikely to give up the chance for a free meal.

Before resigning myself to the dubious safety of my zombie-mobile, I looked toward the ceiling and spotted the heavy chains holding the overhead door in place. Impulsively, I swung the shotgun upward and shot the chains twice. The first shot had been buckshot and wouldn't have mattered if my aim had been perfect. The second slug simply missed the target. I was out of time.

Crap. Crap. Crap!

The first creature had tramped through the gaping entrance and immediately headed my way. I lowered my weapon, aimed, and fired. Puncturing the once-pretty face of a tall, redheaded woman didn't thrill me, but unfortunately, it had come down to a choice between her or me – and since she was already missing her left forearm and a sizable chunk of her midsection, I'd decided to choose myself.

Several more zombies were closing the gap when I lifted the shotgun and targeted the chains again. Luckily, the third shot did the trick, shattering the links to bits. The door slammed down just as more pus-sacks reached it.

A cacophony of pounding and groaning echoed throughout the automotive center as hundreds of zombies collided against the metal door and its four mates, which vibrated and shook so much that I wondered how long they would hold.

I exhaled heavily. "That was too fucking close."

Too fucking close had become my new reality. It sucked but, given how quickly the world had gone to shit, I couldn't imagine it being any other way.

With my latest hurdle cleared, I turned back to the van... and promptly tripped over a corpse. Not the unfortunate redhead. Nope. It was the facedown body of Shaun the former greeter, whose vest had gotten snagged on my vehicle's undercarriage.

Back in the alley, I'd sensed my van was dragging something, but the approaching undead horde had taken precedence. Once I'd screeched into the auto center, I'd been so preoccupied with securing the entrance that I hadn't noticed my unfortunate tagalong – or the bloody, goopy streak he'd left on the concrete floor.

Fan-fucking-tastic. That nasty crap is probably all over my shoes.

Naturally, His Grossness wouldn't be the last infected remains I'd encounter. In the days and weeks to come, I'd likely have to disinfect myself, my duds, my weapons, and the van's interior and exterior more times than I could count.

But for the moment, my priority was getting back on the road – and, ultimately, back to my wife.

So, with a shrug, I unceremoniously kicked the corpse loose and stepped toward the driver's-side door, where I spotted a familiar pair of green eyes staring at me through the barred window. While I'd been dealing with the pus-sacks, Azazel had apparently hopped into my seat and pressed her furry mug against the glass.

"I know, I know." I frowned. "Now, what?"

Yes, I'd managed to escape the zombie horde currently pounding on the metal door like a spastic ten-year-old at his first drum lesson. But my cat and I faced a new dilemma: We were trapped inside Walmart. Actually, we were trapped inside Walmart's auto care center.

I peered around the van and gazed at the sturdy side door leading into the rest of the store. Hopefully, it was unlocked – or at least easy to bust through. If I had to hunker down in Walmart for a while, I wouldn't mind exploring the grocery section for some tasty junk-food treats.

Of course, Clare wouldn't approve of such cravings. Although she shared my penchant for naughty foods, she'd instituted a healthy diet plan (for both of us) in preparation for the impending zombie apocalypse. I understood her reasoning – we needed to be in our best fighting shape to survive the undead invasion – but after all I'd endured since the previous night, I couldn't possibly turn down the chance to swipe some free Ding Dongs, potato chips, or, if I was lucky, a precious bag of Lemonheads.

What can I say? I'm a junk-food junkie.

Prior to the world dying, Clare and I had shared a private joke about my compulsive weakness for snacks. Whenever I'd venture to the grocery store alone and return with chocolate cake, ice cream, lemon poppyseed muffins, or one of our other favorite treats – which pretty much occurred every time I shopped for groceries – my penance was to pout like a kid and mumble, "I cannot be trusted." A silly act that would always make my wife giggle. Mainly because, in all other ways, she could *absolutely* trust me.

But Clare wasn't with me. She couldn't scold me or laugh with me or eat tasty treats with me. I had to overcome my latest trial on my own – or we'd never be together again. And I had to bear in mind that others could be hiding in the store. Walmart, after all, had enough supplies to last savvy looters a good long while – and I hadn't exactly made a subtle entrance.

So, before venturing into the megastore, I reloaded the shotgun and locked up the van. No matter what happened to me, at least Azazel would be safe.

I stepped cautiously toward the side entrance, jiggled the handle, and discovered that the door was indeed locked.

"This shit just keeps getting better," I grumbled.

"Yeah, and I don't think that shotgun of yours will blast its way through," a voice rasped from the other end of the service bays.

Chapter

2

"One-stop shopping: everything you need, right at your fingertips." – Roger, *Dawn of the Dead* (1978)

I whirled around and swung the shotgun upward just as a slender, shaggy-haired white man, maybe in his late twenties, stepped from behind a black-and-gold SUV in one of the adjacent bays. He'd managed to stay quietly concealed all through my loud-ass arrival, which made me wonder how many others presently hid inside Walmart.

But first things first...

For the moment, my priority was keeping an eye on the large bow he gripped in his hands and, more importantly, the arrow he'd pointed in my direction.

Of course, to be fair... I'd also trained my shotgun on him, and unless the stranger excelled at archery, my weapon would cause infinitely more damage.

I gestured toward the bow. "That's different."

He shrugged, then advanced a few steps. "Gotta make do."

I nodded and slowly stepped to my left, trying to put one of the support columns between us. Though the concrete shielded most of my body, I still kept both eyes and the shotgun aimed at him.

His gaze flitted toward my gore-covered vehicle. "Nice ride."

There it is. Dude wants my precious van. Sorry, pal, not today.

"Gotta make do," I repeated, noting his every move.

Smirking, he relaxed the tension on the bowstring and lowered his weapon. Perhaps as a sign of good faith, he even stepped clear of the column's protection. Or maybe he just didn't think I had the stones to shoot him.

True, I still found it hard to kill living humans, but I'd do anything to protect my home and my family.

Including my cat.

After a few seconds, I lowered my shotgun, but left my finger on the trigger. Just in case.

Meanwhile, the zombies continued pounding on the doors alongside the alley, scraping and denting the metal in their ravenous fervor.

"Really riled them up out there," the guy said.

I sighed. "Had no choice. Too many to drive through."

"So, lemme guess. You didn't plan on waiting them out. You hoped to get out that way." He nodded toward the large overhead door on the far side of the Ford – the one facing the parking lot.

And your point is?

Although I didn't appreciate his sarcastic tone, the little prick was right. I needed to shove the compact aside (or barrel through it, if possible), get my ass to the other end of the auto center, and find a way through the front entrance. Hopefully, that part of the property was free of zombies. Or at least less packed than the stupid alleyway.

"Yep. That was my plan."

"Not gonna happen."

I raised an eyebrow, wondering if I should lift the Mossberg as well. Was he threatening me – or simply stating a fact?

As if sensing my thought process, he waved his hand in a conciliatory way. "What I mean is..." He pointed toward one edge of the front door. "See that bolt through the latch?"

I stepped closer, squinting. Sure enough, a heavy-duty bolt lock held the door in place. In fact, someone had secured all the doors – except the one I'd found open – in the same manner.

"Son of a bitch."

I didn't have enough shells to blast through a bolt like that. I needed a key to unlock it. And since I had no idea where to search for such a key – and figured, if it had been in the auto center, the archer would've found it already – I knew we were screwed. Me, Azazel, and the new guy.

He sat on the hood of the Ford Focus, resting the bow and arrow across his thighs. "I know where the keys are."

My gut told me not to trust the guy – not to trust anyone, actually – but since he presently wore a dirty Walmart uniform that seemed to fit his slender frame, I figured he could certainly be telling the truth. On the other hand, he could've been a sleazy looter who'd killed a former Walmart employee, stolen his duds, and gotten himself locked out of the store.

Either way, I don't have many options here.

"OK, I'll bite. Where are they?"

He grinned, as if considering me a hooked fish. "I'll make a deal with you. If you help me get through that door..." He indicated the sturdy, impossible-to-breach door that linked the auto care center to the actual store. "...I'll help you get through that one." He cocked his head toward the front wall.

If the side door were easy to open, he likely would've succeeded before my loud-ass arrival. Frankly, I wasn't sure how he expected me to help him.

What really perplexed me, though, was how he'd gotten stuck in the auto center in the first place – with one of the doors wide-open, no less. I wanted to ask him what had happened, but before I could formulate the question, he continued his proposal.

"My brother's in the grocery section," he explained. "Help me get back to him, and I'll get you the keys."

I didn't fully believe him – about the keys, his brother, any of it – but what choice did I have? At least assisting him would get me inside the store, where I'd have access to tools, food, and other essentials.

"Deal." I extended my hand. "By the way, my name is Joe."

He shook my hand. "Matt."

Same as the name tag on his shirt. Still not evidence of anything more than his ability to read.

"Well, Matt... how the fuck are we gonna get through that door?"

"To be honest, I'm not sure yet."

Cautiously, I followed him to the side entrance: a hardcore steel door that could probably withstand a ton of pressure. As if the powers-that-be had known they might one day face a zombie apocalypse.

Beyond the locked door handle, I also spotted two badass deadbolts that likely wouldn't sustain much damage from a shotgun. An explosive could work, though.

While the van didn't contain any incendiary devices, I was resourceful enough to fashion one from the things I did have – like cleaning supplies and ammunition. I was no expert, of course, but I'd downloaded at least one YouTube video on how to build a bomb from average household items.

Ah, YouTube. Best place for a prepper to get ready for doomsday.

In the runup to our present zombie shitstorm, I'd downloaded a few terabytes of useful how-to videos. Not that I'd had a chance to view them all yet. But I was fairly certain that, in one of them, some psycho had demonstrated the "proper" procedure for building a big-ass bomb out of gunpowder and bubblegum. You just had to grab the video before it was taken down the poster was banned.

Hell, forget this door. I might even be able to blast through the overhead one.

While I reflected on my potential bomb – and how much fun I'd have setting it off – Matt picked up a crowbar and tried to wedge it between the door and the frame. Based on the notches near the hinges, I figured he'd already attempted that maneuver – and obviously failed.

A crowbar couldn't penetrate such a stalwart door any better than my shotgun. Of course, explosives wouldn't work either. If I did attempt to build a Joe-bomb, I'd likely end up blowing myself to hell, leaving poor Azazel trapped in the van, and Clare...

"Fuck. Lemme help you with that."

Matt had managed to squeeze the crowbar in place, so I gingerly leaned my shotgun against the wall – in a spot I could potentially reach before the new guy made a move – and grabbed ahold of the lever. Together, we pulled and pushed on the crowbar, but the damn door wouldn't budge. Not even a little.

With a pissed-off grunt, Matt ripped the crowbar from my hands and hurled it at the wall beside the door, where it left a huge gash in the plaster.

I examined the wall – clearly not as sturdy as the door – then glanced at the Ford Focus. After a few seconds, I retrieved my shotgun and met Matt's frustrated gaze.

"Look, before I get us into the store, I need to know how you managed to trap yourself in here. Who locked you out and why?"

He furrowed his brow, as if insulted by the question, but after a few seconds, realization dawned in his eyes.

That's right. I'm not an idiot. Well, not entirely.

Someone must've had a good reason for banishing him to the auto care center – and leaving him with an unsecured doorway to the outside world.

He sighed with resignation. "When the shit hit the fan on Halloween," he explained, "we... me and the rest of the Walmart employees, I mean... got rid of all the zombies and locked the building down. There were forty-nine of us then."

I had a feeling I'd hear a lot of similar stories in the coming days, months, and years. Every surviving human would have his or her own version of the *it-began-like-this* tale. Some might share accounts of heroism or tragedy, while other, less-noble individuals would try to reframe their involvement in villainous acts to make themselves look better – and get away with more mayhem.

So, which kind of tale is this asshat trying to sell me?

Matt possessed the easy confidence of a skilled storyteller – or a slick bullshitter. The words flowed in a convincing way. In a different life, he might've made an effective teacher – or politician.

"At first, we were all together," he said. "Each department head or manager became the representative for his or her staff, and everyone seemed willing to work toward a common goal: surviving the apocalypse." He sighed. "But all it took was mentioning the store's weapons, and the divide began."

He explained that the Sporting Goods Gang, already in control of the weapons, had wanted to take charge of the food and water supplies as well. Naturally, the Grocery Gang had disagreed, and a battle had erupted between the two factions (with the other departments having taken one side or the other).

Since having the most weapons could determine the victor, the Grocery Gang (the good side, according to Matt) had managed to grab a few guns, some ammo, and over a dozen bows and arrows before having to retreat. The Sporting Goods Gang had nabbed all the rest of the weapons, and the two sides had been at war ever since.

Nothing he said came as a surprise to me. During my journey across New Orleans, I'd witnessed several gruesome scenes of humanity falling to shit and eating its young. So, the fact that gangs could form in less than twenty-four hours didn't shock me.

"What a shame," I said. "If you could've worked together, a store this big and well stocked could've kept everyone alive indefinitely."

For a fleeting moment, his face contorted into one of confusion, as if such a thought had never occurred to him. But he quickly recovered.

"Yeah, it sucks," he agreed. "So, anyway, we secured most of the grocery section. And kept the sporties at bay with our bows." He picked up his weapon. "Not that we're all that skilled."

"Even a poorly shot arrow can poke an eye out," I quipped.

He cracked a smile, then continued his tale. "At one point, I went with the woman in charge of the crafts section to speak with Jason, the leader of the sporties."

"I take it that didn't go well."

He shook his head sadly. "The bastards shot poor Helen. I made a break for it and ran in here to hide, but someone must've seen me cuz they locked the door from the inside, and I had no way of getting back to my crew."

I still wasn't sure I believed his story – especially since I couldn't hear any gunfire or other sounds of mayhem on the other side of the door – but for now, I decided to play along. "Geez, that sucks. How long you been in here?"

He shrugged. "A while. Lost track of time."

"I have to ask... since one of the bay doors was wide-open, why didn't you just leave and try another entrance?"

"Cuz I knew they were all locked." He nodded toward the doorway I'd entered. "The only reason that one wasn't is that someone cut the power before we had a chance to secure it."

"I thought all Walmarts had back-up generators."

An unreadable expression twisted his face, but as before, he recovered immediately.

"Yeah, but the same assholes that cut the power destroyed that system, too." He shrugged. "Guess to make it tougher for us to fight back."

He paused, the pounding, moaning zombies filling the short silence.

"Anyway," he continued, "I wasn't sure how long I could make it on my own. But I didn't think my arrows would last against all the zombies out there. Just hoped someone would free me eventually."

The quiver strapped across his back didn't contain

many arrows, lending credence to his version of the Walmart saga, but still, my stomach clenched with doubt.

As previously mentioned, I'd never liked or trusted most people. Clare, one of the few individuals who'd benefited from my soft side, would playfully scold me for being such a grumpy old bastard, but I knew she appreciated my discerning nature, especially since it balanced out her tendency to trust everyone.

Seriously, maybe the world'll be better off if the zombies win.

The fact was... I didn't trust Matt as far as I could throw him through the plaster wall – which I planned to breach with the stupid Ford Focus. It didn't help that, while he was spinning his bullshit, I'd noticed several grease and oil stains on his dark blue shirt and pants – plus an official patch beneath his name tag that read *Walmart Auto Care Center*.

Nothing wrong with being a mechanic – I'd known plenty of trustworthy grease monkeys over the years. But something about the omission bugged me – perhaps because, knowing the store layout as I did, I realized the automotive section was far closer to the sporting goods than the groceries.

"Please help me," he pleaded, as if sensing my

reluctance. "My brother's still in there, along with a lot of other good people."

No, I didn't trust the guy. But pretending that I did seemed to be my best play for now. So, I'd go along with him but keep my shotgun handy – somewhere only I could reach it.

"OK," I said. "Here's what I'm thinking..."

After explaining my crazy-ass plan to him, I asked him to ready the Ford. Then, while he grabbed the keys from a nearby station and moved the compact into position, I rolled the van closer to my future exit, whispered a few reassuring words to Azazel, and stashed one of my pistols in my pocket.

By the time I'd resecured the van, Matt had emerged from the Ford.

"I don't know if this is going to work," he said, handing me the keys.

He'd given me the reins nonchalantly, but I still sensed he was a smooth operator. Figured he wanted me to drive to keep my hands busy.

No problem. I'll just put the shotgun beside the door and leave the handgun in my left pocket.

I slipped behind the steering wheel. Matt took the front passenger seat. Then I buckled my seatbelt, started the engine, and slowly reversed – stopping only when the back bumper pressed into a lengthy workbench separating two of the bays.

Matt barely had time to secure his own seatbelt before I shifted into drive and, with a rebel yell, hit the gas.

Chapter

3

"I just can't take no pleasure in killing. There's just some things you gotta do. Don't mean you have to like it." – Old Man, *The Texas Chainsaw Massacre* (1974)

A tiny inner voice warned me not to attempt such a dumbass stunt. Behind the plaster might lie wooden studs, concrete blocks, or unyielding rebars that could stop a compact car in its tracks.

But honestly, I was tapped out of ideas. And I sure as shit had no intention of ramming my precious zombie-mobile through the walls of Walmart.

Fortunately, though, I needn't have worried. My crazy plan succeeded – and I had an utter blast crashing through the plaster, breaking two studs in half, and sliding into the hardware department, where I inadvertently caused a deafening avalanche of power tools, lightbulbs, and assorted cans of paint.

What a fucking thrill!

I'd be lying if I claimed otherwise.

Of course, my exhilarating moment of childish elation abruptly ended when several bullets riddled the front windshield and shattered the rear window. I had fleeting glimpses of gun barrels, arrow tips, and ducking heads, but it didn't matter how many enemies had targeted us – just that they seemed to be posted at every possible angle.

"Fuck! They're shooting at us," Matt cried as he ducked below the dashboard.

"No shit, Sherlock." I leaned to the side, kept both hands on the wheel, and tried to navigate through a store lit only by randomly placed lanterns, a smidgen of natural lighting from the front windows, and the old Ford's weak-ass headlights. "What'd you expect? A welcoming committee?"

Before he had a chance to reply, I yanked the car to the left, plowing into a display of car wash detergent. Plastic bottles flew in every direction, and a fountain of blue liquid sprayed the nearby shelves, floor tiles, even our holey windshield.

I would've been better off kicking out the glass, but I had no time for that. I just flipped on the wipers, stomped on the gas pedal, and attempted to ignore the cacophony of shouts and gunshots along the impromptu obstacle course – not to mention Matt's ear-splitting yells.

"Here we go!" I hollered as I maneuvered down an aisle of RV supplies.

More shots rang out, peppering the glass around my head, but I found it hard to accelerate away from the danger. Why? Because the stupid car didn't fit easily between the packed shelves. Naturally, the store builders had designed the aisles with pedestrians in mind, not some idiot driving an ancient piece-of-shit Ford Focus.

When the car finally emerged from the aisle, I turned left onto a wider path, heading toward the front of the store. But almost immediately, I encountered a row of large holiday displays that blocked much of the walkway. Though Halloween had just passed, the staff had already set up its Thanksgiving and Christmas inventory and that crap seemed to be in every bloody nook and cranny!

To avoid a collision, I haphazardly pivoted down another aisle, which seemed even tighter than the first one. The side-view mirrors propelled a slew of LEGO sets, jigsaw puzzles, and board games to the floor, where the car wheels made short work of the cardboard boxes, leaving a trail of puzzle pieces and plastic figurines in our wake.

As I scraped free of the toy aisle, I again turned the wheel toward the front of the store, figuring the wide lane near the checkout counters would be much roomier and easier to navigate. But once more, several giant displays thwarted me.

Fuck! There's crap everywhere! How much stuff do humans need?

I swerved left to avoid hitting an enormous bin of holiday-themed stuffed animals, but the Ford's back end clipped the corner, launching all manner of puffy creatures into the air. Errant bullets blew the stuffing from several plushies, and a ridiculously large elf landed on the hood, partially blocking my view. The windshield wipers failed to knock it off, but we lost our tagalong when I veered into the housewares section, propelling blenders, towels, and other useful items every which way.

Panicked about getting shot – a reasonable fear, under the circumstances – I lost control of the Ford, careened through several carousels of ladies' dresses, skirts, and pants, and ultimately crashed into the store's centralized changing area.

Bullets and arrows permeated the windows, making it impossible for me to hop out long enough to free the Ford from the rubble. Apparently grasping that the ride was over, Matt grabbed his bow, bailed out the car, and bolted through the men's clothing section.

Where the hell's he going?

I needed to follow my fleeing passenger if I hoped to get his brother's keys, but I didn't have the stamina to catch up with him.

For Christ's sake, he's, like, two decades younger than me!

I wanted to take a moment to steady my breath, but my unseen attackers hadn't given up yet.

When the side mirror beside me exploded from a shotgun blast, I knew my time had come to skedaddle. So, I shut off the car, pocketed the keys, grabbed my shotgun, and carefully opened the door.

Whizzing bullets shattered the driver's-side glass as I dove behind a rack of children's socks. After rolling into a low crouch, I lifted the Mossberg to defend myself against the onslaught, but the gunfire had momentarily stopped.

As my heart rate slowed and the adrenaline coursing through my veins dissipated, I reflected on the fact that neither Matt nor I had been hit by a flying bullet or arrow. Pretty amazing, given the odds against us.

But seriously, where the hell is that asshat?

I was staring at a row of girly socks, contemplating my next move, when a shadow darkened the unicorns dancing before me. Instinctively, I whirled around and tilted my gun upward.

Instead of meeting Matt's gaze, however, I found myself looking at the pretty face of a slim, brown-haired woman in her late twenties. Like me, she held a shotgun, which she'd unfortunately aimed at my chest.

Luckily, I didn't fire, and neither did she. For a few seconds, we merely eyed each other, which gave me enough time to absorb the fact that she wore a decent gunslinger outfit over her Walmart uniform. Probably what she'd donned for Halloween.

"Nice costume," I said cautiously.

"Who are you?" she asked, ignoring my attempt at small talk and pointedly keeping her weapon trained on me. "You don't work here."

"Nope. Just passing through."

She cocked her head and pursed her lips, clearly not amused by my answer.

I really need to start reading the room better. Someday, my snark might get me shot.

I sighed, realizing only the truth could set me free. "Look, I have no beef with any of you. I really was just passing through. Using Walmart's back alley to bypass the traffic jam out there. But I got surrounded by zombies and had to pull my truck into one of the service bays. I managed to shoot the door down, just before hundreds of pus-sacks could pour into the auto center, but now I need a key to get out again."

She squinted, as if gauging my honesty.

"Trust me, I don't want to stay here any longer than I have to. I've got to get up to Baton Rouge to find my wife." I sighed again. "So, when I met Matt outside..."

"That no good piece of shit," she growled, tightening her grip on the shotgun.

"Yeah, I don't trust the guy either." Despite my concern that she might shoot me simply for talking to the jerk, I pointed the Mossberg's barrel away from her face – as an act of good faith. "He said he was on the right side of the battle here, but something seemed off. Figured his story was bullshit, but he claimed he could get me out... if only I could help him get back in. And I was desperate." I gestured behind me, toward the crash site. "Hence, the car-shaped battering ram."

Every story had two sides – if not more – and the truth often lay somewhere in the middle. But my gut told me the young woman's perspective would be way more accurate than Matt's slick yarn – and from her disgruntled expression, I suspected she was aching to share her version of the Walmart saga.

She did not disappoint.

"Matt and his gang of thugs tried to take all the supplies for themselves," she explained. "When the madness began, we had almost fifty people in here – and enough food and water to last all of us a long time." She grimaced. "But they didn't see it that way."

"Lemme guess," I replied, "Matt was a mechanic here. So, he rallied the auto department, along with the sporting goods folks and some hardware and electronics asshats, and they decided to grab the guns and any other weapons so they could take control of the store. Probably wanted to kick you and all the crafts, clothing, and grocery people outside, too. Right into the Zombiegeddon."

"Pretty much." She smiled, lowering the shotgun a little. "Course, you forgot the pharmacists. Pets and gardening are on our side, too."

A few shouts and gunshots sounded in the distance, and her grin faded.

"Problem was... my husband, Jason, is the manager of the sporting goods department – and the only one with the keys to the guns."

I lowered my weapon a bit more. "His staff turned on him?"

She nodded sadly. "Bastards. They just ate up Matt's bullshit, not realizing, of course, that he and his piece-of-shit brother are just as likely to turn on them."

"Man, people suck." I aimed the Mossberg at the ground. "Couldn't they have simply broken the displays and gotten the guns anyway?"

She shook her head, lowering her own weapon the rest of the way. "Not anymore. Walmart had a rash of robberies a few years back, so most stores installed shatterproof glass and steel bars. You'd have to pound on it with a sledgehammer to bust through. We didn't give 'em that chance."

"Course, they obviously managed to nab a few firearms. Plus some bows." I nodded toward the rear end of the store. "Got a pretty crazy welcome back there. And come to think of it, Matt seemed surprised they were shooting at him. Now I understand why."

She grinned. "Well, actually, he's been trapped back there for several hours, so he didn't know we'd managed to push his gang out of that area – and that we've been using bows, too. You know, for stealth." A giggle escaped. "But even if those *had* been his folks, they still might've tried to shoot him. Most people aren't all that fond of him and his brother. Frankly, those two have always been assholes."

"What a shocker."

She bit her lip. "Since we're being honest... when we heard the gunfire out there, we assumed Matt wasn't alone. And when the car crashed through the wall, my people probably couldn't see who was inside. Matt's not brave enough to risk a crazy stunt like that, so I'm sure they figured he wasn't the one driving. But just in case..."

"Guess I'll take that as a compliment."

"You should." Her smile morphed into a frown again. "Anyway, our side has most of the rifles, pistols, and shotguns, though Matt and his minions manage to get more every time they kill one of us." She exhaled in frustration. "Taking out the power like they did hasn't helped either."

So, the asshat lied about that, too. Big surprise.

"Jesus," I said, finally daring to rise, my knees creaking mercilessly. "You've got some real Mad Max shit going on here."

She crinkled her forehead, clearly missing the reference. Not astonishing, given that the original movie had come out almost six decades before – and the reboot was already twenty years old.

Gee, lady, thanks for making me feel my age.

"Anyway," I said, "I've got to find Matt's brother."
"Why?"
"Cuz I can't go out the way I came in. Too many hungry zombies in the alley. I need to get my truck – and my poor cat – out through the front of the auto center, and Matt's brother has the keys to raise the door."

Pity flashed in the woman's eyes. Either because I'd admitted to having a cat with me – or because she suspected Matt's brother wouldn't easily relinquish the keys.

But what she said next floored me – though, in retrospect, it shouldn't have.

"Matt's usually got the keys for the auto center."

"Shit. That motherfucker." I shook my head. "I knew he was lying, but I didn't even think to search him. Should've rolled him when I had the chance."

"Sorry," she said, sounding sincere. "He'd do anything to get back in here."

"But wait a second... if he had the keys all this time, why didn't he use them to unlock the door? Or for that matter, why didn't his cronies try to free him?"

The young woman grinned wickedly. "Cuz when we

managed to trap him in there, we didn't just lock it... while some of our people gave us cover, Jason and I nailed a bunch of metal bars across the door. And then bent all the nails into the frame. Since the door opens inward, he couldn't get the damn thing open. We knew he was too big a pussy to try one of the other entrances, and we never allowed his buddies to get close enough to let him out. Frankly, we hoped the zombies would get to him first."

I laughed. "Yeah, that would've been a lucky break."

"Especially since he's the ringleader. Without him, his brother might eventually give up."

Suddenly, I felt guilty – not just naive – for falling for Matt's bullshit. If I'd known what an evil asshole he was, I might've jumped back in the van and let the zombies eat him.

"Well, I'm sorry for ruining your plans. I just wanted to get outta here."

She nodded. "I get it. We're all just trying to survive."

"Yeah, but still... kinda wish I'd killed the jerk when I had the chance."

"You and me both." She extended her hand. "By the way, I'm Jeni."

I accepted the handshake. "And I'm Joe. Sorry again for causing you more trouble."

Her eyes twinkled with mischief. "Help us fight back, and I'll forgive you."

Before I had a chance to reply, a volley of arrows

punctured the shelves beside us. Instinctively, we each dove to the carpet – me to the right, Jeni to the left. I landed near a wheeled display of winter apparel.

Despite my near-death panic, I admit... spotting the puffy ladies' coats made me chuckle. During the decade I'd lived in New Orleans, I'd always found it amusing – Southerners' aversion to cold weather – or, rather, how they'd overreacted to even mild chilliness.

Though Clare had been born and raised in the Big Easy, I'd lived most of my childhood – and adulthood, for that matter – in the North, mainly in Michigan, where residents had been accustomed to below-freezing temperatures and several feet of snow during the winter months. To avoid frostbite, we'd had to bundle up in padded coats and other stifling accessories. Not surprisingly, most kids had lived for snow days – a rare reprieve from school – but weather conditions had had to truly sour for administrators to justify them.

Not so in the South. Requisites differed greatly down there.

I recalled one day, only a few winters before, when it had unexpectedly snowed in New Orleans. At the time, Clare and I had been strolling past the historic French Market, chatting about plans for the holiday season. But soon after spotting the snow, we'd paused to watch the little white flakes dusting the rooftops on either side of Decatur Street.

Lovely, yes. Dangerous, no.

Not enough snow had fallen to accumulate in any significant way. In fact, the flakes had melted as soon as they'd touched the roads, making it seem as though a brief rainstorm had dampened the asphalt – nothing more. Nevertheless, the powers-that-be had canceled school throughout the city.

I shit you not, New Orleans had had an actual snow day – despite any measurable amount of the white stuff. Perhaps officials had worried that bus drivers might get into more accidents amid the sudden snowfall – or maybe they'd just wanted an excuse to play hooky, once a popular pastime in the Big Easy.

Either way, too damn funny.

Of course, what wasn't funny was getting caught up in a deadly battle for Walmart.

Seriously, how do I get myself in such jams?

I crawled along the rough carpet, lugging the display of winter coats behind me. After a few yards, I parked it against a rack of teen jeans, angling it in such a way that I only had to defend one direction. Not that I thought ladies' coats would offer much protection against bullets, but perhaps my enemies wouldn't try shooting what they couldn't see.

As I crouched there, waiting for another unprovoked attack, I scanned the shelves of brand-new denim jeans. Some of them sported the distinctive "torn look" that had first appeared in the 1980s. Dumbest fad ever – one that reappeared every ten to fifteen years.

Yes, humans actually paid for pre-ripped clothes – which I likened to buying a car with pre-stained seats.

I swear, people are fucking sheep.

"Glad they didn't get you," a familiar voice said from a nearby T-shirt rack.

The voice startled me, but I strained to keep my face blank. Matt crouched just above the floor, grinning at me. When I returned the smile, he glanced over his shoulder, clearly watching his back. And apparently trusting me not to blast his front.

If only he'd known my current thought process. Because, yes, I considered shooting him right then and there. I believed Jeni had told me the unadulterated truth. Matt was a lying, murderous piece of shit who deserved a bullet in the head.

Clare had always been amazed by my uncanny intuition – specifically, my ability to figure out people's true motives. Upon meeting a stranger, I could accurately sense if he or she was a selfish, untrustworthy asshole...

Spoiler alert, most people are.

...or a decent person. I'd never been wrong about my initial impression, but I'd often kept my opinion to myself – until the person in question overtly proved me right. Only then would I admit my true feelings to my wife, whose optimism I never wanted to taint with my general mistrust of everyone and everything.

Of course, the zombie apocalypse had tossed the world upside down, compelling even once-noble citizens to behave like amoral psychopaths just to stay alive.

According to Jeni, though, Matt had always been an asshole, so the end of the world had merely given him an excuse to embrace his depraved instincts. While I had distrusted him from the start, I obviously hadn't gone far enough with my initial assessment.

Blame it on the exhaustion.

But now, my people-reading skills told me to pull the trigger on Matt. One thing, however, stayed my hand: the fact that it was possible that he'd stashed the keys somewhere during his mad dash from the car (or if Jeni was wrong and he'd never had them), I'd lose my chance to question him.

Tough to get answers from a corpse.

If I couldn't snag the keys, I'd have to figure out another way to liberate my van, which wouldn't be easy. Without electricity, I couldn't even throw power tools at the problem. And if I couldn't move the zombie-mobile... Azazel and I would be stuck in Walmart – which would totally suck!

So, my best option entailed humoring the psycho long enough to locate the keys and get the fuck out of the store. If I could help the "good" side in the process, all the better.

"Man, this is some batshit-crazy stuff going on here," I said. "Fucking bullets and arrows flying from every direction. Like a bloody warzone."

He nodded gravely. "People will do just about anything when their ass is on the line."

They sure will.

I, for instance, needed to appease a diabolical asshat if I hoped to leave Walmart alive. I just prayed Jeni, wherever she'd hidden herself, would forgive me for buddying up to her enemy.

"Yeah, when you jumped outta the car," I said, feigning dismay, "I worried that our deal was off."

"Nah, man," he replied. "Just didn't want to get shot." He glanced over his shoulder again. "We're in enemy territory, you know."

I peered around the jeans, as if in solidarity against Jeni's group. "So, what's the plan?"

"Well, if we stay low, I think we can use the jewelry area to get back to the grocery section. Left my brother and a few other guys by the bakery."

Apparently, the good guys had taken over the western side of the store, from the hardware section to the garden center, while the bad guys had hunkered down on the grocery side. If the battle lasted too long, I feared Jeni and her husband would run out of food. I wanted to help them, but if I got the chance to leave the premises before the war ended, I had to take it. Clare and Azazel, after all, came first.

With a nod, I scrambled to my feet, bent my knees and back as low as possible, and followed Matt past an assortment of cheap watches and other shiny junk straight off the boats from China. Eventually, we reached a wide aisle and, after peeking in both directions, darted across the gap, into the cereal and coffee section.

Mmm... coffee with chicory.

Even though evening fast approached, a cup of coffee would've hit the spot at that moment. Normally, I alternated between java and diet soda throughout the working day, but since waking up in my courtyard, I hadn't had much caffeine – and unfortunately, pure adrenaline wouldn't sustain me forever.

Naturally, though, I had no time to shop. Just had to focus on my current goal.

Able to walk upright again, Matt and I trekked toward the produce and baked goods near the front of the store – in the diagonally opposite corner from the auto care center.

"It's me, fellas," he said.

At the sound of his voice, a half-dozen men stepped from behind various bins and displays. Four of them carried bows, while two possessed rifles. Fittingly, one of those carrying a firearm sported the same uniform that Matt wore – complete with grease and sweat stains. Given the similar hair color and face structure, I immediately knew it was the ringleader's brother.

Matt turned to me. "Wait here for a sec."

In reluctant compliance, I hovered near the canned fruit while he approached his fellow ruffians. I had no idea what he planned to tell his brother about me – or my van – but I doubted he had any intention of helping me. More than likely, he merely wanted to employ me – and my shotgun –

to assist in his Walmart takeover, and undoubtedly, he planned to kill me and steal my ride once I'd outgrown my usefulness.

Matt whispered something to his brother, giving me the chance to compare their features. They weren't twins – for one thing, Matt seemed a few years older than his sibling – but the resemblance was uncanny.

A glint drew my eye to the brother's waist, where I noticed a set of keys hanging from his belt. So, Matt had told the truth about one thing: His brother really did have what I required.

Good thing I didn't blow a hole in the punk's face.

I needed that keyring to free myself from the madhouse, and as Matt himself had claimed, people would do just about anything to survive.

As he turned, signaling me to join the group, I must've let my poker face slip because his smile morphed into a frown. Clearly, he sensed my hesitation, meaning that whatever he'd told his brother no longer mattered.

And just like that… the jig is up.

Without hesitation, I lifted the Mossberg. My seven adversaries, meanwhile, readied their own weapons. But before any of them had a chance to unleash their bullets or arrows, I scurried back into the cereal aisle and unloaded a round into one of the guys holding a rifle (not, incidentally, Matt's brother).

My blast, which pulverized the dude's torso and sent him screaming to the ground, also blew apart several boxes of dried milk. The powdery eruption gave me just enough cover to bolt down the aisle. At the other end, I turned to the left, aiming for the rear of the store, but a few aisles later, an arrow whizzed past my face, narrowly missing my jaw.

I slipped behind an endcap and peered around the shelves. My attacker, a rotund guy gripping a bow, stood down in the meat section. As he fumbled with his next arrow, I cocked my head, gave him a *what-the-fuck* look, and swung the Mossberg in his direction. I didn't plan on shooting him – not sure I could hit him from such a distance – but when I pumped the gun, he dropped the bow and dove into a vat of unrefrigerated animal parts.

Serves you right.

Given that I'd likely killed one of Matt's pals – and, as a result, his gang was now gunning for me – I probably should've shot the fat archer when I'd had the chance, but instead, I took the opportunity to keep moving.

Part of me wanted to retreat into the clothing section

– maybe even search for Jeni and her husband – but a few more whizzing arrows and bullets nixed that idea. Besides, I needed to stay close to Matt and his brother to get the damn keys.

So, I hunkered down and sought solace in the booze aisle – beer and wine on one side, hard liquor on the other. From the plethora of empty bottles lining the floor, I figured Matt's crew had already downed several adult beverages, and from the streaks of blood everywhere, I assumed they'd murdered at least one person amid the alcohol.

As I crouched against a stack of six-packs, trying to formulate a plan, my gaze fell upon a fallen mop, which someone had clearly used to wipe up some of the blood. Naturally, they'd only managed to smear it even more.

I scanned the shelves around me and spotted one of my oldest brother's favorite brands of bourbon. I wouldn't have minded taking a swig for courage, but given all the crap I'd already endured in one day, I feared a single shot might send me into a coma.

Besides, what I really required wasn't the best liquor – only the highest-proof stuff. The kind that said *lightning* or *moonshine* or *blast* on the label. Before Matt's gang could stop me, I grabbed as many bottles as I could carry and hurled them in opposite directions. Glass shattered, releasing high-octane alcohol all over the tiled floor.

Gunshots sounded from either side of me, hinting that

Jeni's group had joined the current fight. While the good guys kept the bad guys occupied, I readied my shotgun, grabbed the discarded mop, and doused the blood-splattered stringy end with an entire bottle of white lightning. Then, I pulled out my lighter and ignited the alcohol-soaked mop.

In mere seconds, my makeshift torch was fully ablaze and kicking out a fair amount of smoke. As I worked my way toward the end of the aisle, not far from the clothing section, I could hear gunshots, screams, and other sounds of mayhem all around me.

"Motherfucker," a familiar voice shouted from the adjacent aisle. "The bastard's lighting the store on fire!"

"We gotta stop him," a similar voice replied, no doubt that of Matt's younger brother.

Not yet, boys. Not yet.

Careful not to step in any of the puddles of booze strewn about the floor, I scooted to the edge of the aisle just as Matt and his brother darted around the corner. Acting on instinct, I shoved the flaming mop into Matt's face, released the handle, and sent a shotgun blast toward his brother.

While I didn't hit the kid directly, I managed to pepper him with glass and liquor from the bottle I did shoot – something called *Old Man Joe* – which seemed fitting. Having never heard of it before, I just hoped it contained enough alcohol to ignite.

As Matt screamed and clutched his singed face, I reclaimed the flaming mop and swung it toward his brother, who caught fire almost immediately.

Nice job, Old Man Joe.

The young man screamed in pain as the flames licked his face and body. In retaliation, Matt raised a gun he'd obviously concealed from me, but before he could pull the trigger, someone else shot him in the head. He dropped lifeless to the ground.

His brother, meanwhile, had stumbled to the floor, spreading the flames to the large pool of spilled booze. A moment later, the entire aisle was ablaze, blasting heat in my face.

Gunshots echoed throughout the store, and several arrows sailed past my head, from the far end of the aisle. The Battle of Walmart would end soon… and not just because the two brother-mechanics were down for the count, but also because at least three aisles were now on fire.

I hopped over Matt's corpse and gazed down at his brother. He writhed and screamed, clearly still alive.

Quickly, I dragged him away from the flames, grabbed a barn jacket from a nearby rack, and patted him down. His screaming faded as he looked up at me. His face was blackened, and his clothes were shredded, but for having been on fire, he didn't look as awful as expected.

"Thank you," he whispered.

I had no response for him, so I just yanked the keys from his belt and slipped them into my shirt pocket.

Considering all the horrible shit that he and his brother had perpetrated, I toyed with the idea of pushing him back into the flames, but someone else – perhaps the same person who'd executed Matt – did the dirty work for me. A muscular man, roughly my age, lifted the kid and tossed him into the flames, then spit at him for good measure. After offering me a stoic nod, he ran back into the clothing section and vanished into a cloud of thick smoke.

Matt's brother didn't scream or even let out a whimper. He just settled into the flames and burned. A terrible death to witness, but I didn't feel any sympathy for him. And I didn't have time to contemplate my mixed emotions – arrows and bullets were still flying, some toward me but others headed elsewhere.

Hastily, I trekked back through the jewelry department and into ladies' apparel, where I ran smack into Jeni and her husband, Jason. She aimed her shotgun at my stomach, while he targeted my chest with a high-powered rifle. They'd ensnared me – yet surprisingly, neither of them pulled the trigger.

After a few tense seconds, Jeni lowered her shotgun a

few inches.

Course, now it's aimed at my crotch.

Her husband, who stood well over six feet tall (about a foot taller than she was), did not in fact lower his weapon. He kept his gun pointed squarely at my sternum.

I tilted the Mossberg toward the floor and resisted the urge to pull out my loaded pistol. "I've got no beef with you. Just wanna get back to my van and get the hell outta here."

"So you've said," Jeni retorted, clearly pissed.

"Look," I said, "we don't have time to argue. You folks need to get the hell outta here."

"Well, now we do," Jason spat. "Thanks for lighting the place on fire."

"Sorry about that. I was about to be shot. Had to think quickly." I nodded toward the Ford Focus. "Anyway, I still have the keys. If you want 'em."

Slowly, I slipped one hand in my jeans pocket, retrieved the small set of keys, and dangled them between me and the incensed couple.

Jeni lowered her weapon all the way. "Babe," she said, glancing at her husband, "we knew this was never gonna end well."

Begrudgingly, he nodded and let the rifle hang by his side.

With a grateful smile, she accepted the keys. "Did you get the ones you needed?"

Nodding, I patted my shirt pocket.

"Is Matt dead?" she asked.

"Yep... though I can't claim the kill. Someone else took him out before he could shoot me."

"What about his brother, James?" Jason asked. "I hope he burns in hell."

"Trust me, he's burning alright." I gazed back at the ever-spreading flames and smoke. "Speaking of that... I really think it's time to go. Good luck to you both."

With that, I slipped past them and headed toward the auto care center.

Behind me, I could hear Jeni and Jason yelling at the top of their lungs, doing their best to urge any remaining colleagues to vacate the premises.

"The store's on fire," she hollered.

"Everyone needs to get out!" he added.

On-the-nose observations perhaps, but some folks needed an engraved invitation.

By the time I reached the gaping hole I'd left in the wall, the gunshots and arrows had stopped flying. I could hear the revving engine of the Ford Focus far behind me – though it wasn't loud enough to drown out the zombies, still relentlessly banging the overhead doors alongside the alley.

Knowing I didn't have much time, I bolted toward the

front of the auto center and tried almost every key on the ring until I found the right one. Quickly, I released the bolt lock, but before lifting the overhead door, I darted back to the van and unlocked the driver's side – just in case a slew of zombies awaited me in the parking lot and I needed somewhere to run.

Headlight beams flashed across the rear doors of the auto center. Jeni and Jason had obviously turned the Ford around and were working their way toward the giant hole in the wall.

Hoping Azazel was too scared to escape, I set the shotgun on my seat, sprinted toward the front entrance, grabbed the bottom of the door with both hands, and pulled it up hard and fast. I didn't spot a single zombie in the immediate vicinity, though a group of them milled near the far corner of the building. Likely hearing the loud-ass door, one of them turned and noticed me, but luckily, he and his undead buddies were too far away to pose a problem.

I hurried back to the van, secured myself in the driver's seat, and started the engine. Before hitting the gas, I turned toward the murky interior of the van.

"Azazel, baby, are you in here?"

If I left Walmart without ensuring my cat's safety, I'd never live to tell Clare the bad news.

But when Azazel failed to respond, I decided to pull out the big guns. As a New Orleans kitty, she'd always come running whenever she heard jazz or blues. So, I grabbed my phone, opened a folder of downloaded music, and blasted one of my favorite Tab Benoit tunes.

Sure enough, I heard a tiny feline meow, and then Azazel slunk out of the darkness.

"That's my girl."

As Tab continued to play, I drove the van through the service bay, out the open doorway, and into the parking lot. I veered around the zombie horde pouring from around the corner, and a few seconds later, the Ford Focus shot through the bay opening.

Jeni and Jason would live... for now. I hoped their friends would make it, too, but I had to focus on my own survival – and finish the journey to Baton Rouge, where, hopefully, Clare still waited for me.

Seconds later, I exited the parking lot, turned right onto Plantation Road, and looked for an obstacle-free route to Airline Drive. As usual, though, I was probably hoping for too much.

Chapter

4

"Buckle up, Bonehead. Cuz you're goin' for a ride!" –
Ash, *Army of Darkness* (1992)

As lifelong horror, sci-fi, fantasy, and thriller fans,
Clare and I could always find the perfect movie or TV quote
to suit any occasion. Whether funny, sad, or weirdly
insightful, such pop-culture references usually managed to

put even the scariest and most stressful situations into helpful perspective. But I'll admit, not even my favorite shows could've prepared me for the terrifying (not to mention disgusting) shit I'd experienced since the zombie infection had spread to New Orleans.

The day after my first real-world encounter with the undead felt like the longest of my life.

And it isn't over yet.

Since waking up in my courtyard at the crack of dawn, I'd said farewell to my French Quarter apartment and the few neighbors that remained; lugged my poor cat through mobs of zombies to retrieve my wife's diamond ring and our fortified step van; made a perilous, radiator-busting journey across town; and even helped a few deserving folks along the way. Then, after having rescued six ill-prepared yuppies near Xavier University, almost losing control of my vehicle to the ungrateful asshats, and unceremoniously dumping them in the middle of the Earhart Expressway, I'd hightailed my ass west, across the Orleans-Jefferson Parish line, and into Metairie, a sprawling suburb of New Orleans.

Despite my extreme hunger and fatigue, though, I couldn't stop yet. Beating a path out of the Big Easy (my beloved home for the past decade) was only the beginning of my epic battle for survival. The fucking zombie nightmare had truly engulfed the globe, turning average people everywhere into monsters. And not just the undead kind.

If I had any doubts about that, my reluctant participation in the recent Battle of Walmart had proven that the current desperation and insanity knew no bounds.

But no matter what else came my way, I'd need to keep fighting if I hoped to reach Clare in Baton Rouge and safely transport us both to our sanctuary in northern Michigan.

By the time I'd escaped the Walmart parking lot, found my way onto South Clearview Parkway, and finally turned left onto Airline Drive (U.S. 61), the number of meandering zombies had diminished, but the amount of traffic had increased.

As I'd feared, I wasn't alone in my brilliant plan to use an alternate route to escape the city. Many residents who hadn't yet succumbed to the zombie invasion – and who'd instead managed to reach their cars and get the hell out of town – had also opted to avoid the parking lots that vaguely resembled Interstate 10 and the Huey P. Long Bridge.

Shit. Sucks to be us.

Still, the Airline route wasn't nearly as crowded as the I-10 had been earlier in the day. In fact, I was able to travel at almost half the posted speed limit. Although I observed several vehicles slamming into the hapless zombies that wandered across the busy thoroughfare, the traffic, in general, continued to flow.

My progress remained steady for a few miles – until, that is, a horde of zombies stumbled across the road, just past the eerily inactive Louis Armstrong New Orleans International Airport in Kenner. I instinctively lifted my foot from the gas pedal. Surrounding vehicles slowed down, too.

But, naturally, there had to be at least one misguided moron who thought he could simply plow through fifty zombies. While the rest of us pumped our brakes and considered alternate routes, the jackass driving the flashy silver Corvette in the center turn lane actually sped up and made no effort to veer around the unsightly throng. Like the desperate fools in horror movies who attempt to bust through menacing iron gates with their undersized cars, the Corvette driver merely managed to crush a few zombies and stall out atop a layer of carnage.

"Fucking idiot," I muttered, grateful I hadn't attempted the same ill-fated stunt back in the Walmart alley.

With little hesitation, the remaining zombies surrounded the vehicle and pushed against the windows until the driver's-side glass cracked apart. Then, no doubt excited by the motorist's subsequent flailing and screaming, the undead creatures dragged him through the jagged opening and gorged themselves on his flesh, brains, and innards. A horrifying sight, yes, and a small part of me felt sorry for the dumbass, but I'd already witnessed too many awful sights to spare much sympathy for him.

Meanwhile, smart, self-preserving drivers (like me, for once) took an immediate detour off Airline and ventured onto side roads instead.

"OK, Azazel," I said, glancing over my shoulder. "Don't know where you are now, but it's gonna get a little bumpy in here."

Though I'd managed to lure her out of hiding with Tab's soulful tunes, she'd since disappeared again. When I finally had a chance to breathe, I'd need to coax my little scaredy-cat back into her carrier.

Shit. Shit. Shit!

I still hadn't put Clare's grandmother's wedding ring (the one I'd rescued from Troy "the Pimp Daddy of New Orleans" Blanville) back in my wife's jewelry box. While stopped in the middle of the Earhart Expressway, I'd fished it from the smallest pocket of my gore-stained jeans, which lay at the bottom of a garbage-bag-turned-clothes-hamper. But thanks to my unsettling encounter with that weird, vicious, hairy creature, I'd utterly forgotten to store it in its proper place.

Hopefully, I'd remember to do so before I reached

Clare. Otherwise, I might have to answer a few uncomfortable questions – and ultimately reveal certain details of my crazy-ass journey that I'd planned to omit.

For the moment, I needed to focus on the potholes, bodies, and other obstacles in our path – and try not to blow my temper every time the dangling passenger-side mirror banged into the van.

Repetitive noises had always bugged me while driving. Mysterious crinkles, thumps, squeaks, and taps grated on my nerves, and the arrhythmic, metal-on-metal clanging had slowly driven me insane since I'd whacked the mirror on a parking-lot gate in the French Quarter earlier that day. It was especially annoying as I rolled along the uneven surface streets of New Orleans and her suburbs. If Clare had been in the passenger seat, as usual, I likely would've asked her to remove the useless mirror altogether, but in lieu of that, I had to channel my irritation and concentrate on more crucial matters. Like driving and surviving.

Traveling through the neighborhood sandwiched between Airline Drive and the Mississippi River was a completely surreal experience. Like many areas near major airports, it contained an odd mix of houses and businesses – some of which were still smoldering from inconvenient fires and some of which weren't yet devoid of the living. As I wound my way through the varied streets, following other detouring motorists, I'd occasionally spot people peeking out their front doors or windows – residents who'd obviously chosen to stay in hiding, hoping to wait out the undead storm.

Sometimes, I'd spy a few zombies trying to break into a house or storefront – presumably one still sheltering a tasty human or two. Other times, I'd come across a place virtually surrounded by the undead – perhaps twenty decomposing creatures pushing on the doors and windows, likely hoping to find a quick, defenseless meal inside. And sometimes, the living occupants under siege would try to make a break for it. Sadly, most of them wouldn't even reach their vehicles before the ravenous zombies overtook them.

All I (and the other motorists before and behind me) could do was keep driving, our procession of vehicles passing the carnage as if it were just another weekday in the suburbs of New Orleans.

Eventually, we'd wind our way back to U.S. 61 (at that point, officially known as Airline Highway) and then repeat the same detour whenever we'd encounter a group of ten or more zombies. Of course, alternate routes became less frequent in the rural stretch between Kenner and Laplace, so not surprisingly, it took me almost three hours to cover thirty-six miles.

I had a long way to go before reaching Baton Rouge, but unfortunately, I'd noticed the engine was heating up, even with the vents continuously blowing hot air in my face.

My little trick obviously wouldn't stave off the inevitable forever. The van's busted radiator wouldn't survive the rest of the trip to the state capital, and not for the first time that day, I regretted rolling over a broken pipe in the Tremé, just to avoid crashing into a burning, zombified Mardi Gras Indian.

Jesus, I'm sweating my balls off, and for what?

No wonder Azazel had vanished into the back of the van: It was fucking hot up front.

While twilight had descended on the region, and I hated the idea of roaming through a strange town after dark, I knew it was time to take a look under the hood and put my limited mechanical skills to good use. So, I veered south of Airline Highway near Gramercy and weaved through the decimated neighborhoods until I found one featuring several tall, lengthy garages – with twelve-foot-high doors that could accommodate motorhomes, long-haul tractors, and the like. Most of the doors were sealed, but eventually, I spotted an open, empty garage large enough to fit my step van.

"Looks like we finally caught a break, Azazel." I slowed the van and turned into the driveway. "Let's just hope your daddy can fix this damn thing, or we might not be going anywhere for a while."

Though I couldn't bring myself to admit my greatest

fear aloud, I worried the longer it took me to reach Baton Rouge, the less likely I'd see my wife (and my cat's beloved mama) alive again. If Azazel could've spoken English (or I could've understood her feline tongue), she surely would've agreed with me.

Chapter

5

"Well, now that is some fucked-up shit." – Bill Pardy, *Slither* (2006)

From the driver's seat, I stared at the empty garage and considered the situation. My engine rumbled, the only sound in the seemingly abandoned neighborhood, and the hot air still blew in my overheated face. Although I'd pulled into a stranger's driveway, the ass end of my step van remained in the street. I hadn't yet committed to my impulsive plan. For all I knew, zombies or something worse awaited me inside the darkened house.

My eyes flicked down to the temperature gauge on the dashboard. The needle twitched near the red zone. No time to dick around. I needed to make a decision.

Like, right fucking now.

I glanced in the mirrors and through the windows, but except for a few stumbling silhouettes farther up the road, I didn't spot any nosy neighbors. The longer I delayed, though, the higher the probability that hungry zombies or greedy humans would hear my rumbling engine and make a beeline for me. Gazing through the windshield at the gaping garage in front of me, I waited a few more seconds, to see if anyone moved or made a sound inside the attached house, but the former occupants seemed to be long gone.

Or long dead.

So, as the temperature gauge crept into the danger zone, and my van threatened to overheat, I made the obvious call and guided my rig into the garage. I shut off the engine, and once the knocking and rattling had faded, the sudden stillness unnerved me. I even missed the ever-present soundtrack of gushing air through the vents, though I was grateful for the lack of heat.

Despite my whore bath at Home Depot a few hours before, I was once again a sweaty, stinky mess. Also, that morning's headache had returned with a vengeance – no doubt due to my varied injuries and aching muscles, the relentless hot air, and my extreme hunger, thirst, and fatigue. Not to mention the godforsaken mirror, continually clunking against the front right quarter panel. Like my own personal nightmarish version of Chinese water torture.

And now I need another goddamn shower. Fucking perfect.

I turned in my seat, searching the dimness for Azazel, but she'd hidden herself well. "OK, kitty, I'm gonna step out for a minute. If I don't do something about the radiator, we won't be seeing your mama anytime soon."

It might've been my imagination, but I thought I heard a rustling sound in the stillness, and I could swear I saw a shadow shift at the rear of the van. Given her penchant for crinkly paper and plastic bags, it didn't surprise me that my feisty cat had wormed her way beneath the tarp covering my arsenal of guns and other weapons. Of course, it wouldn't have been my first choice for her.

Wonderful. With my luck, I'll get shot in the ass when I try to get her outta there.

I'd rather have coaxed Azazel back into the relative safety of her carrier, but she'd certainly been through enough for one day. As usual, it was wiser to let sleeping tigers lie. Even little tabby ones.

Hell, she had the right idea anyway: snoozing away the stress, fear, dismay, and disgust. I wouldn't have minded a nap myself. But sadly, I had no time for that.

Hastily, I smeared some hand sanitizer on every surface I'd touched since my face-off with the Walmart zombies: the door, the lock, the steering wheel, the shotgun, even my own palms. Then, after chasing a couple aspirin with some diet soda, I gulped down a bit of water, crammed a chili chocolate granola bar into my mouth, and readied myself for more undead chaos. While I alternately munched and swallowed my measly dinner, I loaded the Mossberg with slugs from my backpack, chambered the next round, and slid my door open.

Gingerly, I climbed down from the vehicle and gazed around the dimly lit garage. It was tall, wide, deep, and spacious, with an immaculate workbench and mounted cabinets at the far end, sporting equipment along the sides, and plenty of room for my zombie-mobile.

A muffled rustling drew my eyes to the rear of the van, where I spotted a few leaves scurrying across the bloodstained driveway. The cool autumn breeze that followed them chilled the sweat on my face – a pleasant respite from my stuffy van. But if I didn't have time to nap, then I sure as shit didn't have time to linger in a stranger's garage and savor the refreshing temperature drop.

The sunlight continued to fade outside, and while no person or thing had yet ventured up the driveway, I didn't feel comfortable leaving the door wide open, inviting all manner of trouble inside. Especially since I planned to prop up the hood and delve into the inner workings of my van. The last thing I needed was to hunker down over the engine compartment and be so focused on my radiator that I failed to notice a mob of zombies or looters crowding inside the murky garage and pinning me against the workbench.

From the darkened street lamps and porch lights in the neighborhood, I surmised the electricity was out in Gramercy, just like in New Orleans, her suburbs, and the rest of zombie-infested America. So, I wasn't looking forward to standing in an unfamiliar pitch-black garage – or attempting to release the door from its tracks and close it manually – but safety mattered most. Besides, I had an assortment of flashlights and lanterns in the van.

In fact, I had grabbed a small hand-crank flashlight from my backpack and tucked it inside my shirt pocket. I had a lot to learn about surviving the zombie apocalypse, but at least I was willing to glean a few lessons along the way. I didn't intend to make the same mistake I'd made at Home Depot: entering a strange place without a light source of my own.

Unfortunately, though, I hadn't thought to flip the damn thing on, so as I stepped around the rear of my vehicle and headed for the garage door, I tripped over what turned out to be a solid shadow. Ungracefully crashing to the ground, I promptly smacked my knees against the pavement. In an instinctive attempt at self-preservation, I caught myself with the heels of my hands, but naturally, the shotgun slid from my grasp and skittered down the driveway, along with the useless flashlight that had tumbled from my pocket.

Worse, though, was the fact that something had clutched my ankle. Something moaning and hissing. Presumably the "solid shadow" that had made me fall.

I turned my head and found myself staring at the growling, squinting face of a mangled zombie. Since waking up in my courtyard that morning with a raging headache, I'd learned enough about the undead to suspect the unsightly creature in front of me no longer possessed an active brain. Still, he sure seemed to have more than hunger on his mind. If I didn't know any better, I would've thought he was giving me the stink eye. Considering his current condition, I couldn't really blame him.

While his bloody right hand had managed to ensnare my left ankle, he was the real trapped quarry. His left hand, after all, was lodged between the bumper and the rear of my van, and scanning the rest of him, I realized there wasn't much left below his torso, except the shredded, goo-covered remains of his pelvis. Most zombies wouldn't win any beauty contests, of course, but that one looked as though his lower half had involuntarily gone through a meat grinder or woodchipper.

Although I didn't recognize him, I could only assume I'd picked him up after barreling out of the Walmart parking lot. Not the first disgusting thing I'd dragged into the service bay – that distinction belonged to the former greeter – but a different, much more active zombie.

For all I knew, he could've traveled quite a long distance with me, all the way from Harahan to Gramercy. No wonder I'd received a few bizarre looks from passing motorists. I'd just figured it was the bloody state of the van, not the fact that I'd had an unwelcome, ever-disintegrating tagalong hanging from the back bumper.

Guess it wasn't the leaves I heard a minute ago. Good job, Joe. Way to stay alert.

As the putrefied creature continued to groan, glare, and grip my ankle, a quick glance over my right shoulder informed me the other zombies in the neighborhood had gotten closer. A lot closer.

OK, enough of this bullshit.

I yanked my ankle from the zombie's clutches and scrambled to my feet. I needed to extricate my inconvenient tagalong from the van, but I didn't want to use my shotgun. No need to call even more attention to myself.

I scanned the shadowy garage for an appropriate weapon. With the help of the dwindling sunlight, I spotted a golf club leaning in the corner, next to the closed, pedestrian-only door beside the large retractable one. I sidestepped the disgruntled zombie and picked up the club. Turned out to be a 7-iron.

"Serendipitous," my wife would've said, since that had always been my best club... and her favorite word.

Yes, people, I'm a golfer. Or at least I used to be. Don't judge.

A wave of nostalgia hit me as I gripped the club. I'd been playing golf since the third grade, back when my family had lived in Missouri. So, for nearly four decades of my life, I'd considered myself a recreational golfer. I had countless memories of beautiful spring, summer, and fall days, tackling an assortment of eighteen-hole courses with my friends, my older brothers, and my parents.

A few years before the worldwide zombie epidemic had destroyed everything, I'd even managed to convince Clare to take golf lessons, so we could add yet another pastime to our long list of shared interests. But as with movie theaters and fishing trips, I doubted we'd have much opportunity for golf in the days ahead. Sadly, I'd left all my clubs, even my trusty putter, in our French Quarter apartment. In the end, as much as I'd miss my old life, I could get a lot more mileage from shotguns and other firearms than my golf paraphernalia.

The zombie hissed behind me, and I snapped back to the present.

Fuck, I need some sleep. Ain't got time for daydreams.

Whenever I was having a particularly piss-poor round of golf, I could always count on my 7-iron. I rarely hit a bad shot with it.

To prove I still had a few skills left, I raised the club over my head and brought it down as hard as I could. With a sickening crunch and jolting vibrations in my forearms, the steel head cracked open the zombie's skull, unleashing a horrid, rotten funk, and sunk so deeply into the ooze-covered brain I couldn't retract it. The creature's eyes froze in place, and he groaned and hissed no more.

Quickly, I used a spade to pry his hand from my back bumper, and then relying on the 7-iron, I dragged the body out of the garage and tugged it into the recently mowed lawn beside the driveway. After retrieving my shotgun and flashlight, I scurried into the garage and managed to pull down the heavy door. Just in time to avoid the moaning zombies headed my way.

Chapter

6

"Oh, no tears, please. It's a waste of good suffering!" –
Lead Cenobite, *Hellraiser* (1987)

Using the little flashlight as a guide, I returned to the
van, made a pit stop in my tiny bathroom, and grabbed my
cellphone. Since that morning, I hadn't been able to reach
Clare via text message or phone call, and the silence between

us had really started to weigh on me.

In our more than seventeen years together, we had collectively spent no more than three weeks apart. Most couples we'd known had thought we were nuts for living and working side by side, day in and day out. Pretty much no one could believe we'd successfully done it for almost two decades without driving each other insane. Both of my older brothers had divorced their wives after lengthy marriages, and I myself had gotten a divorce from my first wife, an ill-matched college girlfriend, in my early twenties.

Clare and I were different, though: When we'd said, "I do," we'd meant forever. We often joked that, given how much time we'd spent together, it felt as if we'd been a cohabitating-turned-married couple for twice as many years as we actually had. Equivalent to thirty-five years for most partnerships. And we'd claimed that about ourselves in the best possible way. We were each other's soulmate, best friend, favorite traveling companion, and most compatible partner in crime. I thought nothing – not low funds or health scares or meddlesome mothers-in-law – could tear us apart.

I just hadn't counted on being separated once the zombie epidemic had begun. Given that a friend of mine, far away in India, had warned me about the impending apocalypse and even offered me a timetable for its inevitable spread to America, I thought we'd had more time.

That was how Clare had ended up eighty miles away

from me on the night of Halloween, when the horrendous, zombified shit had hit the fan in the Big Easy. She'd gone to Baton Rouge to fetch her mother, Jill – or at least convince her to escape to northern Michigan with us. I hadn't been pleased with her decision to venture there on her own, but I'd needed time to finish packing the rig, and I knew she'd never forgive herself if something bad happened to her mother, no matter how stubborn, sanctimonious, hypercritical, and insufferable that witch could often be.

But more than thirty hours after Clare had left the French Quarter in a friend's car and more than twenty-eight hours since I'd heard her voice (when she'd called to tell me she'd made it safely to her mother's house), I felt a bit lost without her, like a part of my soul had flown elsewhere. In the time she'd been away, the constant ache of fear and loneliness inside my chest had only deepened.

It had pretty much been the shittiest day of my life. I was fucking exhausted, my rig was busted, perhaps beyond repair (or at least my limited mechanical skills), and I still didn't know if Clare was safe. Or even alive.

True, she'd reached her mother's house, but given how rapidly the violence and mayhem had spread throughout New Orleans and her surrounding towns, I doubted Baton Rouge was any safer. The six yuppies I'd rescued and dumped out earlier in the day had vocalized as much. That had been the reason for the near-mutiny and subsequent expulsion: They hadn't approved of my plan to head to Baton Rouge to rescue my wife, so they'd begun scheming to commandeer my vehicle and venture to the Georgia coast instead. Hence, my gratitude for the gas mask and tear gas canister I'd remembered to stow beneath the driver's seat.

I still had to fix my radiator and find a way to the state capital, but first, I needed to check on my wife again. While I'd forgotten to charge my phone, it still had enough juice for me to dial Clare's number and receive the same irritating message as before. Apparently, the circuits were still fucking busy.

Goddammit.

As an alternative, I tried typing out a brief text to her, giving her my location – and telling her I loved her. Not that either of us had ever questioned our affection for each other; we just said and wrote "I love you" more often than most people. After I hit the *send* arrow, nothing happened for a few moments. Perhaps the phone was searching for the closest network. Any kind of network.

I stood outside the van, in the near dark, staring stupidly at the screen, waiting for the text to reach the love of my life. Finally, I received the *Sent* notification and closed the messaging app. As I did so, I noticed the date on my phone.

What the fuck? It's November second?!

All goddamn day, I'd thought it was November first, All Saints' Day, the day following my first zombie encounter. Apparently, though, I'd lain unconscious in my courtyard for two days, not one. I had spent every lucid moment of the day believing the zombie apocalypse had arrived in the Big Easy only the previous night, when really the terror had come two nights earlier.

Two days and two nights not knowing what had happened to Clare.

Two fucking days and two motherfucking nights!

No wonder the Summers trio I'd helped at Home Depot had given me such strange, mournful looks every time I'd mentioned going to Baton Rouge to pick up Clare. Given how long the zombies had been running amuck, it made sense how little faith Alvin, Ellen, and their granddaughter, Jenny, had seemed to harbor that I'd ever see my wife alive again. Bizarre comments that Troy, the strip club owner, and Marci, the stoned party girl, had said to me earlier made a helluva lot more sense, too.

Still doesn't fully explain the fucked-up scene at Walmart, but whatever. People be psychos sometimes.

As did the overpowering smell of rotting flesh in the French Quarter and the fact that poor Azazel's food and water bowls had both been bone-dry when I'd finally returned to our apartment following my first zombie encounter. My poor little girl had been wandering around our home for thirty-six hours, thirsty, starving, listening to the bloodcurdling screams outside, and wondering where the hell her parents were.

Shit, she really deserves a few bites of tuna. Maybe even a whole can of her own.

My eyes watered, and my chest tightened with every breath. It was even more imperative that I make it to Baton Rouge. Sooner rather than later. Too much time had already slipped by.

With my eyes burning in the near-darkness, I reopened the messaging app and continued staring at the screen. I didn't want to budge until I'd heard from Clare. Even if it was just a quick response to my text. The phone kept searching for a signal, draining the battery even more, but I never heard from her – and I never saw *Sent* change to *Delivered* beside my message to her, so for all I knew, she'd never even received it.

OK, enough fucking around. I need to fix my goddamn radiator and get the fuck outta here.

Pocketing my useless cellphone, I stepped to the front of my van and propped open the hood. Like the heavy garage door, the hood was certainly not quiet. It creaked loudly as it moved upward, but except for the groaning zombies in the driveway, I couldn't hear anything on the other side of the inner door leading into the house. No human footsteps. No zombie moans. Nothing.

Holding my flashlight above the engine compartment, I spotted the problem right away. Even with my limited skills, I could see a sizable hole in one of the hoses leading into my radiator. Not huge, but large enough to siphon away the radiator fluid and cause the engine to overheat.

Crap. Now, what?

During the two weeks I'd gathered supplies for the predicted end of the world, I'd considered food and water stores, medicine, weapons, ammunition, basic tools, batteries, generators, and other essentials, but I hadn't given much thought to radiator hoses. So, while cranking my flashlight to brighten the glow, I took a spin around the garage and searched for anything I could use as a replacement hose. But after a full circuit around the tidy space, searching through every cabinet and drawer and along both side walls, I couldn't find a damn thing that would work. Clearly, whoever had lived there had been smart enough to take any auto parts with them.

Just fucking great.

Chapter

7

"It's not a monster. It's not a monster. It's just a doggy..." – Donna Trenton, *Cujo* (1983)

Since I doubted my van would make it any farther down the road, I had no choice but to search the house for something that could replace the busted radiator hose, if only temporarily. At the very least, I needed the vehicle to carry me, Azazel, and our supplies to Baton Rouge, where I might then have the time and means to find a permanent fix. As a last resort, I could use the duct tape Alvin Summers had given me at Home Depot, but I preferred a more reliable solution, if possible.

So, after resecuring the hood and ensuring I'd locked the side and rear doors of my vehicle (both to safeguard my stuff as well as my cat), I edged toward the innermost garage door, which was accessible via a short staircase. With my Mossberg at the ready, I tiptoed up the six steps, pressed my ear to the wood, and listened intently, but I could still hear nothing on the other side. After a moment of holding my breath, I carefully turned the knob, which was thankfully unlocked, pulled the door aside, and aimed the shotgun forward, the flashlight clutched between my left hand and the barrel of my weapon.

The door had opened onto a cozy utility room, featuring a washer, a dryer, and an extra-deep, free-standing sink on one side and a folded ironing board and a well-organized shelving unit on the other. So far, the house appeared to be as neatly kept as the garage, and luckily, no trigger-happy humans or ravenous zombies had yet to greet me. Of course, my tour of the strange house had just commenced.

Cautiously, I repeated my listening-opening-aiming routine on the second door and soon found myself in a kitchen. Scanning the room with my flashlight and shotgun, I discovered no one living and nothing undead waiting for me. But, unlike the tidy garage and utility room, the kitchen was a downright mess. In fact, so was the adjacent den. Everywhere I looked, I noticed random towels, papers, clothes, toys, framed photos, and other ordinary items strewn across tables, sofas, even the floor. In the harsh glow of my flashlight, I spotted a few overturned chairs as well.

Frankly, I didn't think anyone had looted the house. I could still see a variety of appliances, electronics, and other valuable items throughout both rooms. No, it looked more like the rightful occupants had been in a big, damn hurry to leave.

Given the present state of the world, I could certainly understand such desperation. Not everyone had been blessed with foreknowledge of the worldwide zombie epidemic, and most people wouldn't have prepared for such a ridiculous scenario anyway. Before Halloween, the majority of humans had likely believed zombies were the stuff of graphic novels and Hollywood screenplays. Some survivors were probably still in denial.

An upright picture frame on a ransacked bookshelf caught my eye. It contained a photo of a well-groomed family of five, dressed in their Sunday best. I hoped the man and woman in the image had survived and made it to a decent haven, along with their three kids and the large shaggy dog posing in front of them.

Who knows? Maybe they're some of the lucky ones.

Doubtful perhaps, but anything was possible. I was still alive, after all, and considering how many close calls I'd experienced in the past twelve hours or so, I probably should've died several times already.

I decided to return to the kitchen and search the drawers and cabinets for any item that might serve as a makeshift hose, but as I turned, movement in my peripheral vision drew my focus to the sliding glass doors in the den. Lowering my weapon and flashlight, but keeping my ears alert for trouble, I stepped toward the doors and gazed into the family's spacious, recently mowed backyard.

In the haunting glow of the waning twilight, I spotted an attached deck, which featured an assortment of wicker patio furniture, a sheltered table, and a large barbecue grill. Another short staircase led into the yard, which contained a sturdy swing set, a trampoline, and other kid-friendly items.

For a moment, my mind drifted to thoughts of my own childhood, playing in the yards of our various houses with my two older brothers. Since regaining consciousness outside my apartment that morning, I hadn't spared much thought for my brothers, their daughters, and our parents, all of whom were spread around the country, from Florida to

Chicago. My main concerns had revolved around Azazel and Clare, but I certainly hoped the rest of my family was alright, too.

Naturally, I had shared my friend Samir's warning with all of them, but I doubted they'd believed me. I was, after all, a horror nut with a filmmaking background – not to mention the black sheep of the family. While my parents and brothers considered Clare a bit more pragmatic and definitely more responsible than I was, even her apparent trust in our prepping plan hadn't done much to convince them. Admittedly, the notion of an impending zombie apocalypse was pretty insane, at least in the real world. I just hoped I'd get the chance to see them all again, even if I had to refrain from saying, "I told you so."

Man, I hope they listened to me for once.

Recalling what had drawn me to the glass in the first place, I gazed at the Gothic-style wooden fence enclosing the backyard and, through the gaps, noticed a furry animal on the other side, trying to excavate his way beneath the slats. For an instant, I fretted it was another one of those hairy man-wolf monstrosities I'd seen on the Earhart Expressway – the one that had terrorized the six ungrateful yuppies I'd kicked out of my van. But, while squinting for a better look, I realized it was just a large, familiar-looking dog, similar to my brother James's labradoodle or my parents' long-deceased wirehaired pointing griffon. As if Benji had a bigger, darker cousin.

Apparently, he was trying to pull a reverse jailbreak, digging his way into the yard, not out of it. I suddenly grasped why he seemed so familiar: He didn't merely resemble pets I'd known and loved, he was the actual dog in the family photo I'd recently seen.

Poor guy. He's hoping to come home.

My gaze drifted farther along the fence, and I noticed two zombies stumbling down the rear alley, toward the hapless canine. Given my fondness for horror films, I knew zombie lore varied when it came to non-human animals. In some, the undead ravagers devoured other creatures indiscriminately, from horses to goats, while others left all non-humans with little to fear.

Of course, in the real world, I'd already seen the mangled corpses of assorted dogs and cats in the French Quarter, not to mention the viscera of poor Francis, the resident feline mascot of the Pet Mart. So, I assumed the shaggy canine outside was in grave danger. From the whining and barking I could hear through the glass, I suspected the dog also realized his pursuers weren't the friendly sort. Instead of running from the situation, however, he just carved up the ground more furiously.

"Fuck."

If you knew me at all, then you'd already figured out how I felt about most of humanity. In truth, I believed the planet could've benefited from such a cleansing epidemic at least two millennia earlier.

It wasn't that I had no sympathy for the people who had perished (and continued to perish) in such painfully gory ways. I'd just never had much faith in humanity as a whole. In my defense, men, women, and children had been dying since the beginning of our existence, sometimes at the hands of disease, old age, and Mother Nature, but just as often because of their fellow humans.

The rest of the animal kingdom, however, had always been a different story for me. True, some possessed venomous saliva, carnivorous appetites, and violent urges, but most non-human animals were usually innocent, loyal creatures... until awful humans got ahold of them.

If any cosmic entity oversaw the universe (which I highly doubted), he, she, or it realized I couldn't ignore the present situation. Although I was an omnivore by nature (and, therefore, more than willing to consume beef, pork, poultry, and seafood), my instinct to save or assist any helpless animal placed in my path resonated deep within my soul. Just as with the ill-advised Pet Mart rescue in New Orleans, I usually wouldn't hesitate to risk life or limb for dogs, cats, foxes, elephants, and other non-human creatures, so the anxious canine on the far side of the fence was no exception.

"You better be grateful for this," I mumbled as I unlocked the sliding glass door and stepped onto the deck.

Stuffing my flashlight in my shirt pocket, I hastened down the steps and across the backyard. As I made a beeline for the dog, who was still frantically clawing at the dirt beneath the fence, I surveyed the area and tried to craft a rescue plan. Unfortunately, the fence didn't have a rear gate, and it was too tall, about even with my chest, for me to lean over and pick up the dog from inside the yard. So, as soon as I reached the perimeter, I kicked out one of the narrow wooden slats near the dog. Naturally, the impact of my sneaker on the wood startled the animal, but following a brief glance at me and back at the encroaching zombies, he must've figured I was the lesser of two evils because he resumed his frenzied digging.

Before I could kick out a second slat, however, and grab the dog, I realized the zombies would reach him first. Quickly, I raised the Mossberg and trained the sight on the closest zombie, an obese woman wearing a green apron. Presumably, she'd been cooking a meal when someone had bitten off nearly half her face. As the slug hit her square in the forehead, she slumped to the ground and fell on her back. My eyes, which had adjusted to the dim light, could barely make out the saying on her bloodstained apron: *Don't fuck with me, or I'll poison your food.*

"Hey, what a coincidence," I said. "I've got one just like that."

Clare, grateful for my culinary skills, had given the apron to me as a long-ago birthday present. It was currently stuffed in a kitchen drawer in the step van.

Dammit, Joe. Focus.

Snapping back to the present dilemma, I noticed the remaining zombie, a lanky, decaying man in overalls, leaning toward the dog. Immediately, I kicked out a second slat, grabbed the canine's collar, and tugged him through the opening. Just in time, too. The zombie clacked his nasty jaws where the dog's ass had recently been.

I stumbled backward and landed hard on my own ass. With the collar still in one hand, the shotgun in the other, I tried to recover from the jolting impact, which reverberated from my tailbone to my already throbbing skull. Though the dog beside me trembled with fright, that didn't prevent him from licking my face with wild abandon, obviously more than a little relieved to be standing in his own yard once again.

Grinning in spite of his stinky breath, I turned my head and caught a glimpse of a man watching me through the back door of the neighboring house. I had little time to wonder who he was or what the hell he thought of the scene before him when I heard a ruckus at the fence.

Looking past the dog, I realized the second zombie had knelt onto the ground and stuck his head through the hole in the fence – no doubt in an effort to reach the tasty dog and even tastier (or at least less hairy) man on the other side. Quickly, I released the dog collar, scrambled onto my feet, and aimed the shotgun at the zombie. A few seconds after I unloaded the shell (which, given the short distance, blasted out a three-inch-wide hole through his face), his head slumped forward... onto the barrel of my shotgun.

For an instant, it resembled a fucked-up carnival game in a horror movie.

Get the dead zombie on the rod and win a stuffed animal!

Stepping backward and yanking the shotgun from the zombie's skull, I noted the barrel was covered with chunks of bloody brain tissue and the disgusting black goo I'd come to associate with the undead.

Yeah. I'll definitely have to clean that off.

Meanwhile, the second shotgun blast proved to be too much for the poor, freaked-out dog. Pivoting toward the house, I spotted him bolting up the deck steps and through the open doorway. Before following him, I glanced toward the neighbor's house, but I could no longer see the man who'd been watching me.

Nope, not too creepy at all.

Chapter

8

"No, I don't believe in the Devil. You don't need him. People are bad enough by themselves." – Detective Bowden, *Devil* (2010)

Earlier in the day, I'd learned that sentimentality had no place in the new undead world. Out of misguided respect for one of my favorite aspects of New Orleans culture, I'd impulsively veered around a flame-engulfed, zombified Mardi Gras Indian, promptly rolled over a rusted iron post in someone's yard, and ended up with a busted radiator hose for my trouble.

Unfortunately, though, that was only the first of several major, uber-necessary lessons in the burgeoning zombie apocalypse, and just like the first, the second one hit me like a ton of unwanted bricks: *Don't get distracted.*

Trying to banish the odd neighbor from my mind, I hastened across the backyard toward the open doorway. Although I needed to deal with more pressing matters, I suddenly felt compelled to trail the dog inside his family's abandoned house, worried he might get into further trouble.

Yep, there I was, concerned the dog I'd just saved from zombies would ransack his family's already ransacked home or maybe just endanger himself amid the debris.

I could hear Clare's voice in my head. "Sigh," she would've said. "You're as bad as I am."

I'd nicknamed her Sidetrack with very good reason, and she knew it. Despite well-meaning intentions, she often allowed distractions to derail her focus, which usually made her late for appointments, miss deadlines, or mess up more important issues – and then feel totally guilty about all of the above.

So, given the shifted focus of my one-track mind, I probably shouldn't have been stunned by what happened next. But I was.

As I stepped between the door jamb and the sliding glass doors, I felt the cold, heart-clenching sensation of a gun barrel pressed against my left temple – an impotent moment that would be forever etched in my memory. What a grim fact about the present-day world: Living humans had proven to be more dangerous to me than the goddamn, flesh-eating zombies.

"Drop da fuckin' shotgun!"

Shouting at me from somewhere on my left, the gruff voice no doubt belonged to the asshole holding the pistol to my head.

Figuring I'd end up with a bullet in the brain if I didn't comply, I let the Mossberg clatter to the tiled floor. But, man, how I wished I could've blasted the evil cocksucker with it instead.

"What kinda retard risks his life for a fuckin' dog?"

Now, I really wanna shoot this asshole.

My unknown assailant lowered his weapon, grabbed my left arm, and shoved me face-first against the wall on the other side of the sliding glass doors – not before, however, one of his cohorts flipped on an electric lantern, and I caught a glimpse of three trailer-park rednecks in stereotypical camo outfits. My canine buddy cowered beside a baldheaded joker, who gripped the dog collar in one hand and a semiautomatic handgun in the other. I assumed there were at least four guys in the den, including the mystery man with the pistol.

As my cheekbone pressed painfully against the wood paneling, I tried to calculate my terrible odds of taking them all down, especially if there were other adversaries waiting in the wings. Hunger, thirst, sore muscles, irritating injuries, and extreme fatigue would certainly impair me, but I had no intention of dying at the hands of such assholes. Before I could even attempt an ill-advised counterattack, however, I received a pistol whip to the back of my overtaxed head, which immediately drove me to the floor, onto my bruised knees.

Apparently, my heroic deed in the backyard had made a lasting impression on the dog. Despite my blinding headache, I heard him growl and lunge toward the guy who had just whacked me. The man yelped, cursed, and stumbled away from me, and the momentary distraction enabled me to pivot my torso and survey all four of my attackers.

Three of them appeared to be in their late teens to early twenties. Given their varied hairstyles, vacant expressions, and beefy frames, they seemed like the overgrown offspring of a well-fed Cajun that had crossbred with the Three Stooges. In my mind, I dubbed the frizzy-haired one holding the lantern Larry, the youngest one Moe, and the baldheaded one Curly. Easier than learning their names before they unceremoniously killed me and stole my shit.

I glanced at the man who had pistol-whipped me and was presently swiping at the dog. He definitely seemed older than the other three guys (by at least two decades), and the family resemblance was apparent. No doubt, he was the patriarch of the inbred clan.

Blood splotches and goo splatters covered all four men. Not only their boots and hunting attire, but their faces and hands as well. In a zombie apocalypse, that wouldn't have seemed all that unusual. I myself had dirtied at least three pairs of duds in one day. Still, based on our brief acquaintance, I guessed that some of the blood had come from non-zombies. Safe to assume those assholes had already killed a bunch of innocent people.

I'd thought it many times before: The world had been in serious trouble long before an undead infestation spread across the globe.

Maybe we should just let the zombies have it all. Most humans don't deserve to live anyway.

Although I'd started life as a fairly optimistic kid, my faith in humanity had long since faded. Jokingly, I'd once told Clare I assumed 99.98 percent of the people on the planet were assholes. She might've thought I was kidding at the time, but given that she was a pretty smart cookie and had loved me for almost two decades, I had to believe she knew the truth when she heard it.

Either way, I was certain the four pieces of shit presently threatening me were part of the asshole majority, and I couldn't help but wonder where they'd been hiding when I'd first entered the house. Due to the swampy nature of southern Louisiana, basements weren't as common there as in the Midwest, where I'd spent much of my childhood. So, I doubted they'd come from below.

Of course, they could've hidden in the attic, or one of the bedrooms I hadn't had a chance to investigate before getting distracted by the family pet's dilemma. Given my typically bad luck, they'd likely just happened by the empty house, no doubt in full-tilt marauding mode, while I was in the backyard, rescuing the damn dog.

Whatever the case, they'd likely been attracted by my rumbling engine and the subsequent shotgun blasts. I cursed myself for my lack of situational awareness – and the partial hearing loss that had helped them get the drop on me. No matter who or what was to blame for my current predicament, though, I was fucked and so was the poor dog.

Curly stepped forward and raised a gun to the canine's head. My heart pounded with anger and fright. Abandoned by his family, pursued by zombies, and rescued by a well-

meaning fool, the unfortunate fella was about to die like...
well, like a dog.

"Don't waste da ammo, ya idjit," the older man said.

In reluctant response, Curly lowered his gun, kicked
the dog square in the chest, and sent him sliding across the
tiled floor with a grunt and a whimper. He collided with an
overturned armchair and remained still, just a crumpled pile
of bones and coarse hair. When his sad eyes met mine, he
whimpered again, as if to apologize for his futile act of
revenge – or blame me for his current predicament.

No worries, pup. Don't think I could've done much
better.

"Check da truck," the father ordered Moe.

After turning on a flashlight, the dark-haired kid
disappeared into the kitchen and stomped through the utility
room. His footsteps faded near the garage.

No one made a sound, not even the dog, until he
returned.

"Damn thing's all locked up," Moe reported, then
huffed petulantly.

With my eyes on the kid, I didn't notice his father
edging toward me until he clocked me with the gun again.

Rubbing my sore skull, I looked up into his maniacal
eyes. He seemed to be enjoying the abuse a bit too much. No

wonder his kids were fucktards, too. The bad acorns hadn't fallen far from the vicious oak tree.

"Give him your keys," he growled.

I winced from the blinding pain, then noticed a flat, open palm inches from my face.

For an instant, I considered tackling the son of a bitch to the ground, then remembered how fucking exhausted I was. Not to mention severely outnumbered by his malicious spawn.

"Not gonna ask again," the man said, aiming his pistol at my forehead. "Don't give 'em to me, an' I'll jus' shootcha in da head an' git 'em off your corpse."

As I dug the keys from my jeans pocket and dropped them in the meaty hand hovering in front of my face, a wave of self-loathing crashed over me. Compliance might extend my life long enough to defeat the four idiots surrounding me, but I certainly didn't enjoy succumbing to their demands. Not with Azazel hiding among the weapons that such hillbillies would surely covet – and Clare still waiting for me in Baton Rouge.

The father tossed the keys to Moe, who darted through the kitchen again. Perhaps half a minute passed before I heard the faint but distinctive creaking of my rear doors. Not long afterward, the kid bounded back into the den.

"Holy shit, Paw, it's loaded wit' guns," he said

breathlessly.

If he'd discovered my cache of weapons beneath the tarp, then he'd probably spotted Azazel, too – a fact he would've mentioned to his father. Since he hadn't remarked on seeing a cat, I had to believe that, sensing trouble, my little furbaby must've hidden herself somewhere else.

Smart girl. Smarter than your daddy anyway.

Moe's father grinned, then looked at me. "Well, boys, looks like we hit da jackpot."

Great, just fucking great. Hee Haw and his fucktard kids are gonna get my guns. What else can go wrong today?

"Listen," I said, "the rig is busted, but you can take the rest and go."

Curly stepped forward and kicked me in the ribs, propelling me against the wall. "We'll go when we fuckin' wanna go. Now git your ass up."

With the wind temporarily knocked from my lungs, I had trouble following his command. Exasperated, Curly and the redneck patriarch had to drag me to my feet and pull me across the den, with Moe and Larry leading the way. Glancing over my shoulder, I caught a glimpse of the dog, who'd gingerly raised his head to survey the scene. I lost track of him in the gloom as my adversaries yanked me into the kitchen, through the utility room, and down the steps leading into the garage.

I've had some pretty close calls today, but how the fuck am I gonna get outta this one?

Chapter

9

"People say you should always do the right thing, but sometimes, there is no right thing, and then... well, then you just have to pick the sin you can live with." – Ig Perrish, *Horns* (2013)

Larry's electric lantern illuminated the interior of the garage just enough that, as soon as Curly and his father pushed me against the van, I noticed a narrow gap between the side outer door and the jamb.

"Dammit, Kevin," the father said to the kid I'd mentally dubbed Moe. "Thought I told ya to close da damn door?"

Kevin. Such a normal name for such a waste of human flesh.

The side door beside the large retractable one might be ajar, but not so much that a zombie could've stumbled through the opening without widening the gap even farther. From the father's comment, I assumed the family of marauders had entered the house via the garage. Since the smaller door had been closed when I'd parked my van, I figured they'd arrived after I'd ventured into the backyard.

Strangely, such a notion relieved me. Even though I'd been stupid enough to leave the side door unlocked, at least my situational awareness wasn't so awful that I'd missed the telltale signs of footsteps, murmurs, and breathing when I'd walked through the seemingly empty house.

The kid peered curiously at the doorway. "I did close it, Paw... just like ya told me to."

A new concern popped into my head. Azazel. With at least one (if not both) of the back doors of my van still gaping open, and the outer entrance of the garage ajar, the spry little feline could've easily escaped into the neighborhood. A neighborhood populated by zombies and evil men.

I could only hope the bizarre noises and odd voices outside the van had frightened her enough to persuade her to stay in her new hiding place. As I'd already mused several times since the morning, losing Azazel to death, zombies, or both wouldn't please Clare. If something irreversibly awful happened to our beloved furbaby, my wife would likely leave me, divorce me, murder me, or all of the above.

Kevin's father edged cautiously toward the door and secured it. As soon as he returned to his huddle of sons, I noticed a set of quick flashes from the rear of my van, accompanied by the deafening sound of .45-caliber ammunition exploding from an unseen gun – directly into Larry and Curly's foreheads. As the two older brothers crumpled to the ground, the lantern fell from Larry's loosened grip and rolled under my van.

Even in the low light, I saw Kevin whirl toward me, his gun aimed at my head. No doubt he suspected the mysterious assassin was a friend of mine, but I was as clueless about the person's identity as he was. Not so dimwitted, though, that I hesitated for long. Before Kevin had a chance to pull the trigger, I slammed my shoulder into his sternum, which sent him gasping to his knees and his gun skidding across the concrete.

"What da fuck?" I heard the father shout as he

hurdled over the corpses of his two oldest sons and bolted toward the inner doorway.

Apparently, the big bully was more concerned with his own self-preservation than sparing his youngest son from an untimely demise. Since he surely had no desire to approach the outer door, which stood not far from the concealed shooter at the rear of my van, the utility room was his only viable escape route.

His cowardly move certainly didn't surprise me; he'd likely raised his boys not as a trio of beloved sons, but rather as a band of subordinate miscreants. What did surprise me, however, was seeing the familiar face of the next-door neighbor as he emerged from the shadows. Without making eye contact, he hastened between me and the still-kneeling Kevin, leapt up the steps, and fired off three rounds into the darkness. Based on the grunts and thuds coming from the kitchen, I assumed he'd successfully hit "Paw" – and another round seemed to finish the job.

Meanwhile, a sturdy teenager stepped from the shadows behind my van, pointed his 9mm Glock at the back of Kevin's head, and pulled the trigger. Blood and brains splattered on my clothes as the kid fell forward, but I was too paralyzed to move. For some reason, the only notion that kept circling through my mind was that, except for Kevin, I'd never learned my attackers' real names. How ironic that the four of them had died first, when I'd considered the real possibility that my end would come long before theirs.

Clearly, I was in shock, rattled by the sudden reversal of fortune, fixated on mundane thoughts, and awaiting my own potential head shot. No guarantee, after all, that the enemies of my enemies were indeed my friends.

I was so focused on Kevin's crumpled body at my feet that it took me more than a moment to realize the teenager was standing in front of me, holding the retrieved lantern and staring at me with visible concern. The man, meanwhile, had stepped beside me and squeezed my left shoulder.

"Y'alright, son?"

I turned my head to survey him in the lantern light. Calling me *son* would've seemed odd coming from a man who couldn't be more than fifty, not even a decade older than I was, but he looked like the type that would use his "father voice" with anyone he believed needed protection and comfort. Tall and as solid as a brick shithouse, he had the close-cut hair, no-nonsense air, and practical apparel of a military man. Likely a Marine. And a Cajun, to boot.

Equally well-built, neatly groomed, and sensibly dressed, the teenager looked like a mini-version of the man. No doubt his son.

"Guess so," I said, gazing back at the father. Then, almost as an afterthought, I added, "Thank you. For saving my life, I mean."

"No problem." He grinned. "Name's Ray." He nodded

toward the teenager. "Dat's my boy, Travis."

Ray and Travis both sported a thick Cajun-Yat dialect.
I'd encountered it often during my time in New Orleans, and
frankly, I'd never tired of hearing all the varying accents in
my adopted home of southern Louisiana.

"I'm Joe Daniels."

"Nice to meet ya, Joe," Ray said, shaking my hand
with a predictably strong grip.

"Hey, mister," Travis said, drawing my attention back
to him. He was scanning my van with wide eyes. "Cool rig."
Spoken in a dreamy tone, as if he'd forgotten he'd just shot
someone in the head.

Instead, he resembled his age again, like a boy who'd
seen his first treehouse.

"Would be even cooler if she didn't have a leaky
radiator," I lamented. "And a busted side mirror."

Blood, brains, bone, and zombie goo covered much of
my trusty van, and frankly, it had begun to reek. My shotgun
needed a bit of scouring, too, but first, I had to retrieve it
from where I'd reluctantly surrendered it in the den.

A glint drew my focus to the ground, where I spotted
my keys beside Kevin's motionless hand. I crouched down
and picked them up.

"Hate to seem ungrateful, but I need to check the
van," I said, straightening up. "Make sure my cat, Azazel, is
still inside. I'm afraid all the gunshots might've made her

bolt, and with the garage door open..."

Travis swallowed, his expression sheepish. "Sorry. Dat was my fault. Forgot to shut it when we slipped inside."

I smiled. "You and your dad saved my life. I can hardly complain. But my wife'll kill me if something happens to Azazel."

Just then, I heard padded feet on the steps behind me, followed by a plaintive whine. Turning, I noted the dog I'd rescued standing inside the garage.

"Nice of you to show up," I said. "See you waited 'til the coast was clear."

Ignoring me, the dog trotted past Ray and paused beside Travis. He nudged the boy's denim-clad knee with his nose, until, with an unabashed grin, Travis knelt on the floor and gave the eager pup a vigorous petting.

"Looks like he knows you," I said.

"He does," Travis admitted. "He's Frankie. Da Hamiltons' dog."

"Dis was da Hamiltons' house," Ray explained. "Dog ran away right before dey packed up an' left. Tried to find him, but dey was too scared to stay."

As I'd suspected, the dog belonged there. No wonder he'd tried to dig his way into the backyard instead of fleeing the zombies. He probably figured he'd find safety with his family, but sadly, they'd already left him behind.

"Can't blame them, I guess." My eyes drifted to the

rear of the van, and I silently prayed Azazel was alright. "But I could've never left my cat behind." I glanced back at Ray.

He nodded, plucked the lantern from the floor beside his son, and walked toward the front of my van. "Mind if I take a look atcha radiator?"

"Be my guest."

He seemed like a resourceful guy. Maybe he'd have more luck repairing it than I'd had so far.

Leaving Travis to comfort Frankie, and Ray to peek under my hood, I stepped toward the rear of my van. My chest tightened, as I feared the worst. Most of the time, Azazel was feisty and brave, but as with most dogs and cats, loud noises scared the crap out of her. Fireworks, thunderstorms, rumbling trucks, falling trees, and gunshots usually drove her under the nearest chair or table. But with the van doors and a garage entrance open, all bets were off. Even for a lifelong indoor cat.

Although bustling French Quarter streets and the wildlife-filled woods of northern Michigan had always fascinated her, they'd routinely terrified her as well, enough to keep her furry little ass inside. In fact, except for one time as a brash, three-month-old kitten, she'd never bolted through an open outer door. In the current situation, however, she might've found the outside world less threatening than usual.

Just be hiding in the damn van!

From the rear of the vehicle, I flipped on my hand-crank flashlight and scanned the van's interior. Only a few tense seconds passed before I was rewarded with the sight of two glowing eyes peering at me from the driver's-side footwell.

I smiled, the relief likely evident on my face. "Always knew you were a smart girl."

She blinked once, and I returned the gesture.

"Sorry about the ruckus. I'll try to keep it down. Just sit tight, OK?"

Then I pulled the tarp over my exposed cache of weapons, secured the doors, and strolled to the front of the van. With the lantern perched on my radiator, Ray leaned over the engine compartment, gripped the busted hose, and examined the area for additional damage. When he sensed me beside him, he stepped back from the van, wiping excess coolant from his hands.

"I can fix dis for ya."

"Seriously? That would be awesome."

He nodded toward the side-view mirror. "Can fix dat, too. Course, in a pinch, all ya need is a li'l duct tape."

"Yeah, I forgot a few key items when I was packing up, but luckily, a nice guy back in New Orleans took pity on me and gave me some tape before I left town. Just haven't had a chance to fix it yet."

"Well, ya got a chance now. Hard enough drivin' out dere wit'out bein' half-blind."

"True enough," I said. "But I don't know how to repay you. I already owe you for my life."

Ray gazed at his son, who sat on the concrete floor, surrounded by dead bodies and wrestling with the dog.

"You saved da dog. Dat'd make him yours, but... let Travis take him an' do me one more favor, an' I'd say we're even."

"Looks like Frankie already made that decision for us," I said. "Besides, I don't think Azazel would appreciate him much."

The Cajun dude and his son had saved my life, rescuing me (and my cat) from a bunch of murderous rednecks. On top of that, he was offering to repair my radiator and my side-view mirror. Figured the least I could do was give him the shaggy dog I'd just met and help him with whatever task he had in mind.

I glanced at Ray. "What do you need from me?"

Ray's focus shifted from me to Travis. "Son, go git my red toolbox. An' bring ya li'l sis back witcha. Tell her to pack her 9mm."

"Yes, sir," the boy replied with the discipline of a Marine sergeant. Then, he rose to his feet, approached the garage door, and flipped on a small flashlight.

As he peered through the glass window, no doubt checking for trouble, Frankie scrambled to his feet, too. Obviously protective of his new family, the dog trailed behind Travis and nudged the teenager's leg.

Turning, Travis simply said, "Stay here, boy. I'll be right back." Then, he readied his gun, turned the knob, and slipped into the darkness, shutting the door behind him.

"Wait," I said to Ray. "Should he really be out there by himself?"

"Trust me," he said. "Dat boy know his way round a gun."

Instinctively, I glanced down at Kevin's mutilated skull and recalled how Travis had killed him without hesitation.

Yeah, no shit he can handle himself.

Ray had obviously taught him well — a fact for which I'd be eternally grateful.

Chapter

10

"Trust's a tough thing to come by these days." –
MacReady, *The Thing* (1982)

Frankie sat on his hindquarters a few feet from the
door, fixated on the glass and patiently awaiting Travis's
return.

Ray, meanwhile, surveyed the bodies still lying on the

concrete floor, his expression stoic. Not remorseful at all. Hell, I wasn't sorry either that the assholes were dead.

Better them than me.

Besides, if vigilante justice was ever socially acceptable, I had to believe it was during a zombie apocalypse.

I just didn't think I could've dispatched the rednecks as rapidly as he and his son had. I'd only shot my first man that morning, and even though it had been a clear case of kill-or-be-killed, murdering humans didn't come as easily to me as putting down zombies. Ray, however, was as solid as iron, as sharp as nails, and as accurate as a heat-seeking missile, and Travis seemed to be following in his father's footsteps.

I felt like one lucky bastard, thankful they'd decided to sneak into the Hamiltons' garage when they did. Armed and ready to take out the neighborhood looters. If they'd waited a few more minutes, mine might've been one of the bloody bodies on the floor. My only consolation was knowing I would've stayed dead and not arisen as an undead carnivore.

First, because the rednecks would've likely shot me in the head.

Thanks a lot, assholes.

And second, as far as I knew, you had to be bitten to turn into a zombie. It didn't seem like a situation where a virus lay dormant in every living human, ensuring we'd all turn into zombies after death, no matter if we'd been bitten or not. At least, I'd seen no evidence of that yet. Every zombie I'd encountered so far had sported an obvious wound or missing body part.

All I'd learned from my friends, Samir and Dibya, was that the zombie epidemic had started in their home country – India – and if I'd correctly grasped their reasoning, the infection itself had likely come from "somewhere else," whatever the hell that meant.

True, Myriam Beauvoir – the laundromat-owning voodoo priestess who'd saved my ass in the French Quarter – had mentioned a place called the Infernal. But seeing as how I'd never heard of that before, I couldn't automatically assume that *somewhere else* and *the Infernal* were one and the same. Especially since the details of the epidemic's origins were still nebulous at best, and with Samir and Dibya likely long-deceased, I certainly couldn't ask them for a better explanation.

Someday, perhaps, someone would uncover the real facts of how the whole end-of-the-world crisis had begun, but for the moment, all I needed to know was that the zombie infection had spread around the globe and that I had to stay alive long enough to protect my feline spitfire and see my beloved wife again.

I glanced at Ray. "Did you know those guys?"

He shook his head. "Not from aroun' here. We saw 'em go into several houses 'long da street. T'ought about droppin' 'em den, but dey was only goin' into empty places."

I nodded in understanding. Why risk his life, and those of his kids, to stop some armed looters? Though tempted, I refrained from asking why he and his children had opted to stay behind in the first place when most (if not all) of their neighbors had already fled. They seemed more practical and resourceful than that – the type of streetwise survivalists that would've had a bug-out site in mind.

"But den Travis saw 'em enter dis house," Ray continued, "as you was savin' da dog out back."

I waited for a smart-ass comment about putting myself at risk for a damn dog, but it never came. Regardless, I almost opened my mouth to justify myself (and what some might think was a misguided preference for animals) by saying that pets could become zombified creatures, too, and ultimately turn on their families, but I hadn't actually witnessed that yet. So far, dogs, cats, and other non-human animals appeared to be just more fodder for overactive, ever-present undead appetites. And after the corpses I'd already seen in the French Quarter and elsewhere, I couldn't have stomached watching poor Frankie get eviscerated by those

two zombies. Especially since he reminded me of my parents'
old griffon, Gypsy – the finest dog I'd ever known.

"Knew we best git over here before dey didya in," Ray
admitted.

*Well, ain't that something. Saved several times today
cuz of my love for animals.*

Once the gunshots had stopped ringing in my ears,
and I'd realized my new pals had no intention of killing me
as well, I'd briefly wondered if rescuing Frankie had saved
my life. I gazed at the dog, who still stood by the door but
had pivoted himself around to watch me. For a moment, I
held his eyes, long enough to convince myself we shared a
mutual understanding and perhaps even mutual respect. I'd
saved him from the zombies, and he, in turn, had spared me
from the rednecks' bloody fate via the neighborly
intervention of Ray and Travis.

Suddenly, Frankie shifted his focus beyond me and
unleashed a guttural bark. Alarmed, I whirled around and
noted Azazel's face, forepaws, and upper torso in the
passenger-side window. She'd apparently climbed onto her
carrier, leaned against the glass, and spotted Frankie in the
shadows with her impressive night vision. Of course, she was
hissing and grunting at the strange if friendly-looking dog.
And Frankie, who stood on all fours in a protective stance,

was growling in return.

Sighing, I turned to Ray. "See what I mean? Taking Frankie was never a possibility."

Ray chuckled, then frowned. "We best calm 'em down, or dey'll lure ev'ry zombie in da area."

I certainly didn't want such an outcome, not the least of which because Travis and his little sister still had to navigate their way back to the Hamiltons' garage. In the dark, no less.

So, while Ray clutched Frankie's collar, I carefully slid open the driver's-side door of my van, stepped inside, and scooped up Azazel before she had a chance to wonder what I had in mind. Gently, I guided her inside the cat carrier, and naturally, she cried with displeasure as I secured the gate. To placate her and distract her for a while, I opened a can of tuna, spooned about a third into a porcelain ramekin, and slipped it through the little lid atop her carrier.

As expected, she stopped meowing immediately and dug into her favorite treat. I stroked her furry head, tucked the remaining tuna in the fridge, shut the carrier lid and the van door, and rejoined Ray near the dead looters.

"Oh, shit," I said. "I forgot those idiots left the back door wide open when they grabbed me."

Hoping the barks and gunshots hadn't enticed any unwanted visitors into the Hamiltons' house, I retrieved my trusty axe from the passenger-side footwell in my van and led Ray up the steps, over Paw's bullet-riddled corpse, and into the den. By the light of the lantern my companion carried, I didn't see any zombies inside the house, but I could certainly hear a few undead interlopers moaning along the rear fence. Without hesitation, I shut and locked the sliding glass door, then picked up my shotgun from the tiled floor. Felt good to hold the Mossberg again, even if the barrel was still covered in zombie foulness.

After performing a quick sweep of the rest of the house, we returned to the garage. While we awaited his children, Ray briefly related the tale of how he, Travis, and his daughter, Nicole, had returned from a fishing trip on Lake Maurepas to find the boat launch overrun by decomposing carnivores. Although he didn't strike me as a fan of horror movies, he matter-of-factly explained how he'd encountered and dealt with the sudden zombie epidemic. Obviously, he didn't care whether his enemy was an Iraqi insurgent or an undead corpse; he'd handle either situation with the same precision and determination.

As I'd assumed, Ray was a former Marine. He'd dedicated more than two decades to the service and would've done so for the rest of his life – if only his wife hadn't gotten cancer, forcing him to retire earlier than planned. After she'd died, Ray had willingly raised his children on his own, teaching them all he knew about defending their home, property, lives, and loved ones.

So, naturally, all three of them had been armed, even his daughter, on their shocking return to the boat launch. A few well-placed head shots, and they'd reached their truck and made it home more safely than most people surely had.

Based on his accent, I'd also assumed Ray was a native Cajun, and I was right. Raised on the bayous of southern Louisiana as a shrimper and a gator hunter, he'd returned to his fishing and hunting heritage during his retirement. But he'd obviously kept up with his shooting practice and physical conditioning, too.

Shit, the dude couldn't be more of a badass if he tried.

He certainly put my own attempts to prepare for the zombie apocalypse to shame. While I'd spent the past two weeks gathering supplies, walking twice a day, and learning how to use my varied firearms, I was still overweight, out-of-shape, and nowhere near ready for such a species-ending challenge.

I glanced down at the bloody floor of the garage. Just as I wondered whether Ray and I should stack up and cover the bodies of the dead looters, Travis returned with his little sister and his father's toolbox.

I'd worried that the sight of the three corpses would upset the young girl, but perhaps not surprisingly, she turned out to be as tough and imperturbable as her father and older brother. Roughly three-foot-nothing and maybe seven or eight years old, she marched right up to me, stuffed her Glock in a side holster, and thrust out her hand. Despite her small stature, she had the same black hair and no-nonsense vibe Ray and Travis possessed.

"I'm Nicole," she said.

With a wry grin, I accepted her hand and shook it. Her grip was almost as firm as her father's. "I'm Joe. Nice to meet you, Nicole."

Ray, meanwhile, took the toolbox from Travis and placed it on the workbench. Dents, rust, and even what resembled dried blood marred the large red box. It looked as though it had already endured an apocalyptic event.

"Four more zombies walkin' out front," Travis reported to his father.

"Recognize 'em?" Ray asked.

"T'ree of 'em were so messed up I couldn' tell, but one was definitely Mrs. Kerry."

"Damn, dat's a shame. She was a nice lady."

A moment later, Travis and Nicole were sitting on the ground, petting Frankie without a care in the world, and their father was once again examining my engine compartment.

"So, where ya headed wit' dis rig?" he asked me.

"Well, first, I have to make it to Baton Rouge, to pick up my wife, Clare," I said. "And then we're headed to northern Michigan."

With any luck, my parents would be up there, and if

possible, I intended to collect my brothers, John and James, and their daughters along the way.

Ray squinted at me like I had lobsters (or, more appropriately, shrimp and crawfish) crawling from my ears. "Why ya wanna head all da way up dere?"

"It's a pretty isolated location, and I've been sending stuff up north to prepare for this."

"Prepare for dis? For da dead to rise?"

"It's a long story, but a couple weeks ago, some friends of mine told me this was gonna happen. People I trust. Not many of the folks I told believed me, of course, but well, I guess my friends turned out to be right."

Briefly, I explained what little I knew about how the zombie infection had begun in India and eventually spread to New Orleans. I still had some questions about the whole thing, but Ray took my story in stride – despite its obvious holes. He might not have trusted me had I shared the same news two weeks earlier, but nowadays, seeing was definitely believing. In the end, it didn't really matter how the zombie chaos had started. All us survivors could do was deal with the rotten consequences and try to... well, survive.

Nodding stoically, Ray turned back to his beat-up toolbox, opened the lid, and revealed a neatly arranged assortment of tools. After a quick search, he grabbed a slotted screwdriver, a box cutter, a stainless-steel duct clamp, and a roll of thick black tape.

"I told you, I have some duct tape," I said, edging toward the passenger-side door of my van. "Hate to use up all your stuff."

"No problem," he assured me. "Got a ton of it. An' it's a helluva lot sturdier dan duct tape."

Without awaiting my response, he reached into the engine compartment and pulled off the busted hose leading into the radiator. Even though the van had been cooling down in the garage, I'd pushed her to her limit, so I wasn't surprised to see steaming antifreeze coolant pour from the radiator and the hose. The radioactive-looking green shit was surely still hot to the touch, but the guy didn't even flinch.

Yep, definitely a badass.

Using the box cutter, Ray sliced the holey end off the hose, then wrapped the rest of it with his heavy-duty tape. He slipped the duct clamp onto one end of the hose, forced the hose onto the radiator fitting, and tightened the clamp with the screwdriver. In less than a few minutes, he'd fixed my ride.

"It'll need some more antifreeze," he said, "but for now, we can jus' fill it back up wit' water."

I nodded, figuring I'd swipe some water from the Hamiltons' toilet tanks or, if it had cooled down enough since the blackout, their hot water heater. While I hadn't provided for every occurrence during my frenzied two-week prep phase, I'd made sure to fill my van's built-in and portable water tanks. But there was no point in wasting my own supplies. Although my parents' Michigan property curved around a freshwater lake, had access to a well, and was equipped with a couple generators (thanks to my maxed-out credit cards), I wanted to make sure we had enough water for the long journey north. There was no guarantee we'd encounter handy resources along the way – or folks as generous as Ray and his kids.

Turning to my latest savior, I simply said, "Thanks, Ray. I really owe you."

"Don't mention it."

With my assistance, he then proceeded to repair my side-view mirror. I held it in place while he taped the shit out of it. It wouldn't last forever, but unless I ran into any more parking-lot doors, it would likely hold until I could replace it in Michigan.

"So, lemme git dis straight," Ray said when we'd finished. "Ya bought all dat stuff, but didn' git a good set of tools or spare parts or even some duct tape?"

From most people, such a question would've come across as *you're a fucking idiot*, but Ray seemed to be genuinely asking me. I felt foolish admitting that I'd left several rolls of tape behind during a recent supply run to Home Depot – and that I'd forgotten to remove my own tools from beneath the backseat of my pickup truck when I'd sold it to purchase the step van. So, I merely shook my head. What else could I say?

Smirking, he shut the toolbox lid and slid it toward me across the workbench. "Take dat. Got more tools dan I know what to do wit'."

"I don't know what to say," I said, dumbfounded by the guy's generosity.

I was tempted to ask if the non-rust stains on the toolbox were indeed blood, but thought better of it. Assholes might've made up 99.98 percent of the world's population, but Ray and his children were certainly part of the .02-percent contingent, and I didn't want to repay his kindness by insulting him.

Ray lowered my hood, then turned back to me. "An' now... 'bout dat favor."

Chapter

11

"You know the part in scary movies when somebody does something really stupid, and everybody hates them for it? This is it." – Trish, *Jeepers Creepers* (2001)

"Dere some folks trapped in da offices on da second floor," Ray informed me.

We were lying precariously on a rooftop in downtown

Gramercy, using two pairs of Ray's night-vision binoculars to scope out the Sacred Heart of Jesus Catholic Church on East Main Street.

Clare and I weren't religious by nature; in fact, we were both atheists. Still, that had never stopped us from harboring a fascination for religious history and architecture. As Catholic churches went, however, the Sacred Heart wouldn't have impressed either of us.

No St. Louis Cathedral, that's for sure.

An understated tan brick building, it sported narrow stained-glass windows, a porte-cochère, and a solitary steeple. At the moment, however, its most notable attribute was the fact that it appeared to be filled with and surrounded by zombies. Loads of them.

Climbing onto our current perch hadn't been easy, but it would've been a lot tougher with hungry zombies in the vicinity. I'd been grateful for the lack of mindless carnivores nearby, but looking through the binoculars, I understood why that had been the case. It seemed as though most of the town's former residents were trying to cram their way inside the church. Not for solace or salvation, but perhaps out of habit – or more likely because of the tasty morsels on the upper floor.

Through the binoculars, I could see several people milling about a darkened office – just as Ray had claimed. They weren't stumbling around the room like zombies but pacing with nervous anticipation. Like living humans in major trouble.

"Uma an' Eunice were workin' up dere when dis all happened," Ray explained. "Deir husbands fought deir way into da church, but dey ran outta ammo... Been dere ever since. Dey managed to reach me on an ol' shortwave radio, an' before you showed up, I was tryin' to figure out how to git to 'em."

Shifting the binoculars from the office to the parking lot beside the church, I realized the zombie horde was almost as huge as the one I'd faced at the French Quarter party house earlier in the day. Well, to be honest, I hadn't faced them. I'd fled from them, along with a couple of lucky stoners.

Hours later, my new pal Ray hoped I'd help him bust some of his neighbors out of a zombie-infested church. It was fucking suicidal, and we both knew it. If Ray hadn't saved my ass, I doubted I would've agreed to assist him. As far as I was concerned, putting my life at risk equated to putting Clare's life at risk, and I refused to fail the love of my life. At least more than I already had.

But, even though I'd hoped the favor Ray needed was

less life-threatening, I certainly couldn't turn down the man who'd spared my life, my cat, and my ride from a nasty end.

After Ray had repaired my radiator and mirror, he'd explained that he required my help in rescuing some friends from a nearby church. I'd realized then why a pragmatic guy like him had waited to flee the neighborhood. He had more people to save.

So, after filling the radiator with toilet-tank water, I'd wiped the zombie goop off my shotgun, secured the toolbox in the storage space beneath my sofa bed, and given Azazel some more well-deserved tuna. Then I'd fueled myself with a handful of cashews and dried cherries (thinking, at my current rate, I'd be at my pre-marriage weight in no time) and hauled Ray, Travis, Nicole, and Frankie to a curved driveway that lay at a relatively safe distance from the zombie-infested church.

Presently, I lowered the binoculars and turned my head. "So, what's the plan?"

In response, Ray glanced over his shoulder. I figured he was checking on his kids, who stood with Frankie outside my parked van, several yards behind us. Honestly, I thought he might suggest we take them and the dog back to his house before embarking on our suicide mission, but from his next question, I realized he wasn't looking at them.

"What kinda guns ya got in dere?"

Although he'd caught a glimpse of the uncovered

weapons when he'd awaited his chance to take out the rednecks, he'd been a bit preoccupied at the time. Now, he could focus on a more critical mission – one that would require as many firearms as possible.

So, after a brief discussion about my stash, we scrambled down from the roof, ventured back to the kids, and laid out the necessary arsenal in the rear of my van: two fully loaded shotguns, a couple of 9mm handguns, two machetes, and plenty of ammo. I also had a couple of ARs under the sofa bed, but Ray figured, with the low light, we'd be better off with the shotguns.

Before we'd left the Hamiltons' house, Travis had run back home to fetch a duffle bag filled with some of the family's best weapons. Presently, he unzipped it and removed a bolt-action sniper rifle. According to the boy, he hadn't owned it for long, so he was still learning how to handle it.

"Dat's a Barrett M98B," Ray informed me.

While the designation meant nothing to me, I had actually heard of the company. I'd spent the last couple of weeks, after all, learning as much about guns as I could.

"Da boy's got a few udder rifles, too," Ray elaborated, "but dey not designed for what we gotta do."

Admittedly, I was afraid to ask for details. Regardless of the plan, there was a good chance one or all of us wouldn't survive the night.

Well, Joe, shit's definitely about to get real... Hope I don't press my luck this time.

Chapter

12

"There's too many of them. I can't kill the world." –
Reverend Harry Powell, *The Night of the Hunter* (1955)

"Seriously, this is batshit-crazy," I mumbled as Ray
and I pulled away from the abandoned house where we'd left
his kids and the dog.

He'd obviously raised some tough offspring, but when

he'd told me that Travis would stay behind with the sniper rifle and little Nicole would "spot" for him, I thought he might've overestimated their capabilities. Still, I'd refrained from contradicting him as he and I steadied a ladder against the side of the empty house – a house situated between two trees, with a gently sloping rooftop that offered a clear view of the church and its adjacent parking lot. I'd stayed quiet as Travis and Nicole scurried up the ladder with their weapons, a pair of night-vision binoculars, and a couple of my walkie-talkies. I'd even kept mum as Ray climbed to the rooftop with one hand, hauled Frankie with the other, and then helped me and Travis slide the ladder onto the roof, just above the gutter (where no zombies or marauders could reach it, but the children could still access it in an emergency).

With the kids serving as a lookout for us, we readied the guns and other weapons we planned to use during the rescue attempt, and I finally took the time to divvy up some of my arsenal between the crate under the tarp and the storage space beneath my sofa bed. Then, perhaps to dispel any unvoiced concerns of mine (and to verify his own assumptions about his children's skills), Ray surveyed the church with his night-vision goggles and used one of my remaining walkie-talkies to instruct his kids to take out two of the zombies shuffling along the edge of the parking lot.

Nicole, gazing through the binoculars, spotted the

first one and called it out to her brother, who immediately took the head shot. Peering through Ray's spare goggles, I saw the zombie fall to the asphalt. When Nicole indicated the second zombie, I watched as it, too, tumbled to the ground, motionless.

"Wow, he's good," I said, shifting my focus toward the rooftop, where Travis and Nicole awaited further instructions, and Frankie calmly sat beside them, either already used to the sound of gunfire or unwilling to abandon his new family. "Not that I had any doubts."

Ray grinned. "Sure ya didn'."

"Hell, why don't we just sit back and let your son pick 'em off one at a time? Less suicidal that way."

Ray frowned. Maybe he didn't think putting all the weight of responsibility on his children's shoulders was the best approach. Instead, he explained, "Don't got an unlimited supply of ammo for dat gun, so Travis'll only shoot when we need him to."

I shrugged. Made about as much sense as everything else I'd done that day. And honestly, I didn't feel like arguing. I'd already wasted more time and energy than I'd intended in my effort to get to Clare. In retrospect, I likely would've reached Baton Rouge hours earlier, had I not decided to reclaim my wife's ring, avoid the flaming Mardi Gras Indian, and stop to help people in need. At the moment, I had just enough reserves left to assist Ray, get back on the road, and hopefully reunite with my wife.

I drove down North Millet Avenue, turned right onto East Second Street, and eased the van down Church Street, which, as the name indicated, led directly to the Sacred Heart of Jesus Catholic Church. Luckily, the church had a small parking lot and a circular driveway that passed beneath the porte-cochère, which was doubtlessly intended for staff members and parishioners to be deposited right at the door and protected from inclement weather. Unfortunately, it wouldn't safeguard them – or us – from the hungry zombies lumbering in and out of the open doorway.

I paused near the edge of the parking lot, the night-vision goggles displaying the horde of zombies along the driveway and up to the building. The way they were milling about like lost lambs drawn to a familiar place (much like those wandering in and out of the Whole Foods Market back in New Orleans) would've been laughable, if it wasn't so terrifying.

My gaze shifted to the office windows, where, via the goggles, I could see several men and women peering down toward my vehicle, which they could likely hear but not see exceptionally well. All the nearby street lights were out, and I'd purposely refrained from flipping on my headlights to keep from drawing too much undead attention to myself. Unfortunately, though, my rumbling engine already had that covered. While the bulk of the zombies were either inside the church or peppered along the driveway, several of those in the parking lot had shifted in our direction and headed toward the van.

It's now or never.

I took a few fortifying swigs of diet soda, turned in the driver's seat, and spotted Ray standing a few feet behind me, holding a couple of bungee cords. "Are you sure about this?" I asked him.

With a wink, he simply said, "We got dis." Then he moved toward the rear of my van and opened both doors.

While Ray hopped onto the asphalt and quickly linked the bungee cords from the back wheel wells to the rear doors, to keep them from closing during the mayhem, I glanced toward the front passenger seat, where Azazel still lay curled and safe inside her carrier. Though tempted to cover it with a towel, as I'd done before chasing the yuppies from my van with the tear gas canister, I was afraid she'd be even more frightened if she could hear the gunshots and moans, but not observe what was happening.

As if proving my point, I heard the report of two rifle shots, in speedy succession, and turned my head just as a pair of zombies fell right in front of my van. Travis and Nicole were clearly keeping an eye on the situation and trying to prevent the undead from reaching us. Suddenly, I felt grateful for leaving them behind on the rooftop.

Once Ray had braced himself at the rear of my van and gave me the green light to proceed with Operation Batshit-Crazy (my words, not his), I stepped on the gas pedal and headed toward the enormous group of undead in and around the main entrance of the church. Rolling along the circular driveway and honking my loud-ass horn, I collided with a tall male zombie sporting a bloody, gooey stump where his right arm had once been (presumably before another zombie had gnawed it off). I drove too slowly for the impact to destroy him, but as he fell, my wheels crushed his legs, so I knew he wouldn't be going anywhere, at least with any speed.

On my first pass beneath the porte-cochère, he was the only zombie I managed to snag. To be fair, I wasn't trying to hit any of them. Ray's plan merely required me to drive past the horde and lure the undead away from the church entrance. Hence, the honking horn.

Even before I turned around on Church Street and circled back through the narrow driveway, we had accumulated a trail of eager zombies. Ray started letting loose with the shotgun, blowing through undead heads with the extreme efficiency you might expect from a badass Marine. Once the first shotgun was empty, he picked up the second one and continued shooting.

By the time we'd made our sixth pass around the

circular driveway, he and his sniper son had put down nearly forty zombies, and I'd crushed a few more beneath my wheels. Sadly, though, we'd barely made a dent in the undead population, and between the horn and the gunshots, we'd only enticed more zombies from the surrounding neighborhood.

A much bigger problem, however, was that our little merry-go-round, shoot-'em-in-the-head scheme had gotten far less productive. While I crept along at fifteen miles per hour around the driveway, plenty of zombies had continued to follow the van, but many more had either ignored us on their way inside the church or spread across the driveway and the nearby parking areas.

Inconveniently, we'd also created several piles of gore, and on more than one occasion, my wheels had slipped and lost traction amid the bloody body parts left in the wake of our shooting and driving. Finally, when I hit a large bump (which could've been a torso, a couple of skulls, or something worse) and Ray lost his balance, toppling over backwards in the van, we both figured it was time to start Operation Batshit-Crazy, Part Two.

Chapter

13

"If you say, 'I told you so,' I'll shoot you." – Detective Jim Lipton, *Dead Silence* (2007)

Ray regained his footing in the rear of my van as I rolled forward, straddled Church Street, and hit the brakes. We only had a few moments before the undead mob would engulf us from all sides. I watched over my shoulder as my current partner in crime set down his shotgun and plucked two grenades from his backpack. Then I shifted the van into reverse, backed up toward the entrance, and stopped several yards away.

The horde of zombies still looked to be at least ten bodies deep outside, pressed against those already inside the church, like drunken Bourbon Street revelers on Mardi Gras Day.

Except, you know, more likely to tear your face off than simply vomit all over you.

Ray pulled the pins from both grenades and tossed them toward the open doorway. I promptly hit the gas and pulled forward, just as a few zombies bumped into the sides of my van. A few seconds later, two ear-splitting explosions blew a ragged, bloody passage through the undead blockade, shook the entire edifice, and crumbled part of the foyer. I'd seen grenades go off before, but never quite like that. The detonations were massive, accompanied by enormous fireballs.

Where the hell did he get those fucking grenades?

I knew Ray had been a longtime active Marine, but holy shit, I sure could've used a few of those things in my own zombie-killing arsenal. The closest I'd come was following an online video about making your own pipe bomb.

Before the flames and smoke had a chance to dissipate, gunshots echoed across the parking lot. Travis had opened fire at the entrance, taking down as many zombies as humanly possible, many of which were still inside the church.

"Go. Go. Go!" Ray yelled as he started to reload the shotguns.

Taking my cue, I slammed the van into reverse and headed toward what remained of the church entrance. As the vehicle rolled over an assortment of nasty, undead body parts amid the rubble, my usually ironclad stomach churned a bit at the nauseating sounds of thunks, cracks, and squishes beneath my wheels.

Travis, meanwhile, kept shooting any and all zombies he and his sister could spot inside and immediately outside the church, only pausing to reload. Fortunately, he stopped altogether once I'd pressed the rear of my van against the doorway. After all I'd endured in the last fourteen hours or so, it would've been a shame to die from friendly fire.

I unbuckled my seatbelt and got to my feet. With the goggles, I could only see about half a dozen zombies still in the partially destroyed foyer. I'd parked us so close to the gaping doors that none of the undead creatures in the parking lot would be able to squeeze inside. Good thing, too, since we had no idea how many zombies were waiting for us throughout the rest of the church.

Azazel chirped, and I gazed down at her through the slits of her carrier.

"You're staying here, little one. I'll be back in a few."

Then, before second-guessing myself, I draped a towel over her carrier. Although I hated to leave her alone in the dark, I really didn't want her to witness the chaos outside the van. Although many people would've disagreed with us, Clare and I had never viewed Azazel as merely a cat. To us, she was our little girl, and we were often very selective about what she saw, heard, and experienced. If we weren't comfortable having sex when she was in the bedroom with us, then we sure as shit didn't want her watching zombie brains and guts spurting all over the place.

As I approached the rear of the van, Ray tossed me my Mossberg, hopped down to the ground, and ventured into the church. By the time I joined him, he'd already finished off three of the nearest zombies.

"Git dat one," he said, nodding to his right. "'Member, only head shots count."

I almost spewed a smart-ass quip like, "No shit, Sherlock. Tell me something I don't know," but I refrained.

Instead, my eyes followed his gaze toward the wall, where I spotted a small table filled with flickering votive candles. It seemed odd to see such a peaceful tableau amid all the chaos, but obviously, the folks trapped in the church hadn't had a chance to blow them out yet. They'd no doubt had other priorities – like surviving.

I aimed at the back of a teenage boy, who was dressed in a baseball uniform so caked with blood and zombie goo that I could barely discern the team sponsor who'd provided his jersey. The logo of Don's Bail Bonds received a full-on blast as my shotgun sprayed out, propelling the boy against the side table.

"Shit."

Given my ongoing hunger, fatigue, and headache, I wasn't terribly surprised when the shot didn't finish off the zombified kid, but I was still embarrassed in the wake of Ray's advice about only targeting undead brains. Before I could correct my mistake, however, some of the candles tumbled onto the boy, and he caught fire. Typical of my ongoing bad luck, he scrambled to his feet, whirled around, and stumbled toward me.

Fucking terrific. A repeat performance of the goddamn, flaming Mardi Gras Indian in the Tremé.

In the time it took Ray to shoot the other two zombies, the former baseball player had set one side of the foyer ablaze. I shot him again, this time in the forehead, but it was too late. I could already feel the heat of the flames. The fucking church was gonna burn.

"Crap, we need to hurry," I told Ray. "No way we're putting this out."

The two sets of double doors leading into the rest of the church were presently closed, but based on the shuffling and moaning sounds coming from the other side of the doors, I assumed they'd been open at some point during the zombie apocalypse. Along the walls on either side of me stretched several benches, but unfortunately, the flames were encroaching upon the ones on my right.

Before we lost the opportunity, I spluttered out an idea. "Maybe we can create a corral of benches around the doors on the left, prop them open, hop over the benches, and let the zombies inside the church fill the corral. Then, if there aren't too many of them inside, we can slip through the doors on the right and seal off the corral from inside the sanctuary." I beamed, quite proud of my zombie battle tactics.

Ray turned toward me, his night-vision goggles making it difficult for me to discern his expression. "But we gonna be trapped inside," he countered. "We won't know how many more zombies in da corr'dors an' stairwells, an' we might not find anudder way to git out."

He might've shat on my brilliant idea, but he hadn't yet deterred me. "If this fire spreads, we won't be able to use this exit anyway."

As Ray stared at the flames, shaking his head in dismay, the dire truth hit me.

Fuck. This fire's gonna consume my van.

Ray must've read my mind because he turned to me and said, "OK, look, we do ya plan. Only you drive off an' try to lead 'em away. Da van can't git caught in da fire."

"Fucking right, it can't. No offense, Ray, but that van means survival for me and my wife. Besides, Azazel's still inside."

He nodded, seeming to comprehend that I wasn't being a coward. I had proposed an idea, after all, to penetrate the sanctuary. I just hadn't considered all the consequences. No way I'd endanger my precious zombie-mobile – or my beloved cat. Not even for a bunch of hapless humans trapped upstairs.

Before the flames could make the decision for us, we shifted all the benches between the two sets of double doors, creating a barrier that, once we opened the left-hand doors, would guide the zombies through the flaming foyer, out the church, and after me. I was relatively comfortable with the plan; I'd already played the role of Demented Pied Piper of New Orleans back at Home Depot.

Just hope I survive my encore.

Chapter

14

"Come and get it! It's a running buffet! All you can eat!" – Shaun, *Shaun of the Dead* (2004)

As previously stated, I'd never been particularly religious, and neither were my brothers. Once my oldest brother, John, had gotten his driver's license, he'd started taking me and James to the arcade in lieu of church on

Sundays – and none of us seemed to suffer from the deception.

Still, I felt somewhat guilty for setting fire to a Catholic church in Gramercy. That certainly hadn't been my intention when attempting to put the zombified baseball player out of his misery.

Ah, well. Shit happens.

Luckily, I spotted a silver lining. With the wall ablaze, I no longer needed the constricting night-vision goggles to see.

Before the flames reached the dark burgundy curtains hanging from the only two windows in the foyer, Ray and I ripped them from the rods and secured them above the double doors on the right. A moment later, Ray stood behind the curtains, his large frame mostly hidden from view.

As soon as I opened the left-hand doors, nothing but a bunch of benches and two pieces of dusty, antiquated drapery would separate my new friend from a horde of impatient, ravenous zombies. I stared down at his boots, the only things presently showing. I felt bad about leaving him behind in a burning church, but when I heard Ray pump his shotgun, I snapped out of my momentary daze.

The guy truly had balls of steel. I only hoped that was enough. First and foremost, I wanted him to live through our crazy-ass rescue effort. But I couldn't deny my second realization: If Ray died in there, Clare and I would be stuck with his kids, which wouldn't be ideal for any of us.

Don't get me wrong: I loved my nieces, and I didn't hate children in general. But Clare and I had never really wanted human kids of our own. More than anything else, we were cat and dog people – though Clare wouldn't object to having a pet otter someday, and I wouldn't mind adopting the elephant that I used to play catch with at Potter Park Zoo in Lansing, Michigan.

So, basically, the badass Cajun Marine needed to fucking live. At all costs. For him *and* his kids.

To help the cause, I even dragged a few of the dead zombies closer to the curtains – in lieu of covering Ray with zombie gore. I hoped the collective smell of the rotting undead would mask his fresher, more enticing scent from the ravenous creatures about to invade the foyer.

"Ready, Ray?"

"You bet," came the muffled reply.

I moved around the barricade of benches, approached the doors we had "fenced off," and grabbed one of the handles.

"Now," I yelled as I yanked open one of the doors.

Jesus Fucking Christ, we are so hosed.

It only took one glimpse at the sanctuary to recognize there were a lot more zombies inside than we'd originally thought. Of course, it required the actual creatures much *less* time to realize a human meal stood in the open doorway.

"Good luck, Ray," I yelled as I darted along the benches and clambered inside the back of my van. "There's a shit-ton of the fuckers!"

Rapidly, I moved toward the driver's seat and tossed my shotgun and goggles onto the floor. I'd left the back doors of my van wide open, having surmised the zombies would be more likely to follow me if they could smell me.

OK, maybe I'm not the smartest zombie battle tactician.

Like an idiot, I hadn't even thought to start the van and leave the engine running before opening the sanctuary door. And naturally, when I turned the key in the ignition, nothing happened. My chest tightened, and beads of nervous sweat popped out along my brow. In a panic, I kept turning the key. Still, nothing.

Son of a bitch.

Although I'd made a lot of expensive improvements to my delivery-truck-turned-zombie-mobile, she was still a fairly old vehicle. After all she'd already endured, perhaps her crapping out was inevitable. I just wished she could've waited until we'd reached our family compound in northern Michigan. Especially since I could hear a herd of zombies moaning and shuffling not far behind me. With the rear of my vehicle pressed against the foyer, the only place they could funnel was into my fucking van.

I took a deep breath, attempted to calm my nerves, and turned the key again. Apparently, the fifth time was the charm. The van fired up, and I immediately hit the gas pedal, flipped on my headlights, and cranked the steering wheel to the left.

While Ray and I had been busy in the church, several zombies had cautiously neared my van – probably enticed by the possibility of food but, like Frankenstein's monster, too scared of the flames to get too close. Unfortunately, though, they were currently in my way. Without hesitation, I whacked into several of them and crunched over piles of carnage as I rolled along the circular driveway. My poor van would be hell to clean, but at least I had escaped certain death.

Glancing over my shoulder, though, I noted I wasn't completely in the clear. Backlit by the flaming foyer, several zombies darted toward the van, and one of them managed to grab ahold of my rear bumper. Clad in dirty overalls and clearly missing his lips, he tried to claw his way inside.

I jolted the van to the right, hoping I could shake him loose as I veered around the driveway, but he was one determined fucker. As I turned onto Church Street, a gunshot pierced the darkness, and when I looked back to check on my tagalong, I noted the zombie's entire head (not just his lips) was gone. I was still dragging the body behind the van, presumably because his arm was caught in the bumper, but at least he could no longer try to kill me. Another shot rang out, the arm exploded, and the body tumbled into the street, leaving only a hand and part of a forearm flopping in the cool night air.

Scratch what I thought. Adopting Ray's kids would be like having a small army. That kid's an amazing shot.

Once the immediate danger had passed, I slowed down to fifteen miles per hour again and started to repeat my earlier routine: honking the horn and driving around in a circle, along the driveway and Church Street and back again. Unfortunately, however, I no longer had a badass ex-Marine with a shotgun in the back. So, I had to keep glancing awkwardly between the windshield and the rear, to ensure no zombies climbed aboard.

As I made my second circuit around the driveway, I noticed quite a trail of undead creatures behind the van. By the time I'd made my third trip past the burning church entrance, I could still make out the open doors leading into the sanctuary, but I could no longer see Ray's boots beneath the flaming curtains. Although it pleased me to think he hadn't been eaten or burned in the fire, I knew, from the sound of gunshots inside the sanctuary, that not all the zombies had vacated the church. In his effort to shoot as many as possible, Ray hadn't even had a chance to shut the doors, as he'd planned.

Abruptly, I heard a beep coming from my shirt pocket. Someone was signaling me via my walkie-talkie. Either Ray or the kids.

I removed the device from my pocket and turned up the volume. "This is Joe. Go ahead."

"Almos' to da offices, but we gonna hafta leave t'ru a top-floor window. Too many downstairs for us to handle. Over."

I pressed the *talk* button. "I'll get the kids. Then if you can get everyone out the windows and onto the lower roof, I think I might have an idea."

I turned onto Church Street before remembering walkie-talkie protocol. "Over," I added.

"Gotcha," Ray replied. "Talk to ya in twenty. Out."

I took one more pass around the driveway, to see if I could lure a few more zombies away, and then gunned it down Church Street. When the undead creatures following my van failed to catch me, they quickly lost their enthusiasm and headed back to the church. I could only hope the flames were enough to deter them from reentering the building and pursuing Ray upstairs.

As I retraced my route down East Second Street and North Millet Avenue, it occurred to me I no longer had hot air blasting in my face. With all the preparation and excitement of the past hour or so, I hadn't had a chance to enjoy the simple pleasure of driving without having to worry about the radiator. Based on the gentle snoring inside the covered carrier, Azazel was grateful as well – or else, she was too exhausted to give a shit.

Chapter

15

"I came here to do something. So, we are gonna stand around, or we are gonna do something?" – Pillsbury, *Land of the Dead* (2005)

As I pulled alongside the house where Ray and I had left Frankie and the kids, I could see Travis and Nicole were already packed up and waiting for me near the edge of the roof. After helping them lower the ladder to the ground, I braced it as they scurried downward, and together, the three of us waited for Frankie to leap down onto the roof of my van.

I glanced at the kids. I didn't have to tell them their dad was still inside the church, working his way toward the offices. They had one of my walkie-talkies, so they'd heard his last report with their own ears.

Most children would've freaked out over the idea of their father being trapped inside a burning church, surrounded by flesh-eating zombies. But not those two.

True, Nicole didn't look as carefree as most girls her age. Though she stood several feet from my headlight beams, she seemed paler than when I'd met her in the Hamiltons' garage. Still, even at eight years old, she remained calm. No tears yet shed.

Naturally, I was delighted to see her smile when Frankie leapt from the roof of my van into my extended arms.

I huffed. "You're heavier than I expected. Thought you were more hair than muscle."

Frankie licked my face in response, and Nicole actually giggled.

Then, there was Travis, who, at fourteen years old, already behaved like a seasoned Marine. As soon as I set Frankie inside the van and detached the bungee cords from the rear doors, the boy helped his sister climb aboard, slid their gear across the floor, and kept watch while I clambered inside. With impressive speed and agility, he followed me into the van, closed one door, and reached for the other one just as a random zombie (no doubt attracted to the lights and gunshots) careened around the corner of the house and took a swipe at him. Without hesitation, Travis pulled his pistol from his hip holster, put a bullet right through the creature's left eye, kicked the corpse to the ground, and then closed and locked the back door.

Fucking kid's as hardcore as his old man.

Before any other zombies could stumble upon us, I shut off my headlights, donned the night-vision goggles, and reversed over the dead zombie. As I backed onto North Millet, the walkie-talkie beeped again.

For how little they'd cost me, the devices had a pretty decent range. During the two weeks I'd spent readying for the impending apocalypse, I'd often relied on the recommendations of other RVers and doomsday preppers. The purchase of my four walkie-talkies had directly resulted from one such recommendation, and as with many of the essentials I'd bought, I was exceedingly grateful for other people's expertise and willingness to share information... even if most of the folks with whom I'd corresponded hadn't believed me about the zombie epidemic and were likely dead.

"Sitrep," Ray said. "Over."

I stopped the van, squinted at the walkie-talkie, and then looked over my shoulder at Travis, who sat with his sister at the dining table.

He chuckled at my confusion. "Situation report," he explained.

While I'd often heard the term *sitrep* in various movies and TV shows, I'd never actually used it or even looked up the definition before. That was the sort of thing Clare usually did.

Nicole giggled again, and I felt my cheeks flush with embarrassment.

I continued toward East Main Street, pressed the *talk* button, and said, "Hi, Ray. Frankie and the kids are in the van, and we're back on the road. We'll be there in a minute. If you can bust out those windows facing the parking area, I can pull the van alongside the church, and you can all drop onto my roof. Over."

Luckily, the survivors were huddled inside an upper office overlooking the rooftop of a single-story addition to the building. If they could find something to break the glass of the two slender windows I'd mentioned, they might be able to escape before the entire fucking church burned down around their ears.

"Sound good," Ray replied. "Only one problem... we

got an injured man up here. Over."

Crap.

If by *injured*, Ray meant the guy had a zombie bite, the situation had become a lot more complicated.

"Maybe you could lower him down first," I said, "and then the rest of you can hop down. Over."

"Might jus' hafta carry him myself. No matter what, we'll bust out da windows now, so we be ready. Over an' out."

I neared Church Street and removed my goggles.

Good news: The flames have spread, so I don't need the goggles anymore. Bad news: Uh, well, the flames have spread.

"What's wrong, Mr. Joe?" Travis asked.

What isn't?

But I spared him the thought and instead asked, "What do you mean?"

"Ya frowned when my dad said someone was injured."

Real nice poker face, Joe.

Despite the goggles, the kid had still read me like an open book. With ridiculously large print.

"I'm not sure," I stalled. "Let's just get your dad and the others outta there before the whole damn church burns down."

I turned onto Church Street and stopped the vehicle.

Shit.

It looked as though even more zombies had amassed outside the burning building. Either the intense glow of the spreading fire had lured more of them to the scene or the heat of the flames had chased others from inside the church. Either way, the rescue wouldn't be a cakewalk.

So, here was the actual sitrep: Ray and his pals were currently on the second floor of a burning church, the front third of which was engulfed in flames. Zombies poured from the dilapidated church entrance. Many of them were on fire, but as with the Mardi Gras Indian, that hadn't stopped them yet. I was planning to drive right through the horde, across the lawn, not far from the office windows, so that Ray, the super Cajun Marine, could help lower a bunch of trapped people onto the roof of my home-on-wheels. Before we all burned to death or got ripped to bloody pieces.

OK, seriously, how do I get myself into these fucking

situations?

In a fifteen-hour period, I'd encountered more deep-shit scenarios than I had in all of my forty-five years on the planet. And I was still about forty-five goddamn miles away from the love of my life.

Chapter

16

"Run for it? Running's not a plan! Running's what you do once a plan fails." – Earl Bassett, *Tremors* (1990)

While surveying the bizarre scene, I couldn't help but wonder... if the eyes of a zombie on fire melted away, would it still be able to sense fresh meat nearby?

Normally, I would've said that zombies could smell

living humans even better than they could see and hear them. But many of the undead creatures presently stumbling across the circular driveway, grassy lawn, and parking lot were rather preoccupied. In fact, at least half of them seemed to be ablaze. Silhouetted by the flaming church behind them, they were flailing their limbs, swiping at each other, and banging into their fellow undead creatures like steel balls and plastic flippers in a malfunctioning pinball machine. Naturally, they also happened to be spreading the flames to other hapless zombies.

So, the fact that the fire was baking their eyes down to the size of shriveled grapes and rendering the orbs absolutely useless was the least of their troubles. I doubted, too, their aural and olfactory senses were topnotch at the moment. The overwhelming odor of charred, rotten zombie flesh assaulting my nostrils likely hampered their own ability to sniff out me and the kids in the nearby van.

I wasn't sure yet if the limited brain functions of the undead included pain reception, but they certainly moaned as if the fire hurt them.

Man, I hate that fucking sound. Don't think I'll ever get used to it.

Of course, only half of the zombies wandering around the church were on fire, which meant the other half had their full sensory functions. As soon as they spotted my van on Church Street, they promptly rammed themselves into the front and sides of the vehicle, which rocked from the ongoing assault. No doubt, they were also smearing their gross zombie goo all over my beautiful baby.

Yep, I said *beautiful*. Beauty had always existed in the eye of the beholder, and to me, my zombie-proof step van was as gorgeous as a swimsuit model.

Well, almost. But in a zombie apocalypse, the van'll take me and Clare much farther than a hot chick would.

Before the undead could completely surround us, I resumed moving forward, knocking over the zombies in my path, crushing their body parts beneath my sturdy wheels, and trying to avoid the flaming ones at all costs. As I approached the designated pickup point, I saw glass spray out from one of the upper windows. At least someone was still alive up there. Hopefully, it was Ray.

Glancing over my shoulder, I was again amazed at how calm and well-behaved his children were. As stoic as his father, Travis quietly slid off the built-in bench and stepped toward the front of the van, likely for a better view through the windshield. Meanwhile, all color might've drained from Nicole's face, but she didn't make a peep.

In fact, the only one making any noise, besides the

undead horde on all sides, was Frankie. He didn't tremble. He didn't bark. But as he'd demonstrated with the zombies near the Hamiltons' back fence, he seemed to know those outside had nefarious intentions. With his bird-hunting nostrils, he could surely smell the death and decay, so it was no surprise he'd braced himself in fighting stance beside the table. Every time a zombie jolted the van, his hyper-aware eyes widened, and he released a low growl, his teeth bared. I suspected that, if a zombie slipped aboard my ride, Frankie would know exactly what to do with those teeth.

A badass dog for a badass family.

I turned toward the passenger seat and pulled the towel from atop Azazel's carrier. I hated leaving her in the dark for too long. To her credit, she merely peered at me through the narrow slits, but refrained from her usual chirping or crying. She was either too scared or too tired to say much of anything.

Shifting my focus back to the windshield, I said, "Keep an eye out for..."

Before I could finish my thought, though, Travis interrupted me. "Mr. Joe, my dad jus' tossed a rope outta dat window."

I followed his gaze to one of the upper office windows. It didn't appear to be a rope – more like a chain of knotted tapestries. Something assembled in a hurry. I just hoped it would hold as my soon-to-be passengers ventured down the church roof and onto my van. I also hoped no one was too overweight – not because I fretted about the sturdiness of my roof, but because it would be difficult to squeeze a fat ass through such a narrow window. Crude as it sounded, we simply didn't have time to grease someone out of a tight spot.

It had already taken longer than planned to push through the zombies in the parking lot, across the lawn, and alongside the church. Although I managed to plow through most of the overly eager creatures, many others slipped beneath the vehicle and became little more than zombified speed bumps.

When the van was only a few yards from where I planned to stop, a heavy chalice sailed across the roof of the building, bounced onto the hood of my van, and left a sizable dent behind.

"Goddammit," I grumbled as I slammed on my brakes.

I wasn't pleased about the latest dent, but when it came to zombie-mobiles, functionality mattered more than cosmetics. Besides, it amused me that desperate times had called for sacrilegious measures. I doubted anyone in the soon-to-be-burning office cared that the chalice had once held the sacramental wine during Holy Communion. When survival mattered most, even devout Catholics were willing to sacrifice religious relics to break the thick glass covering their only possible exit route.

"Uh, Mr. Joe..."

Travis's concerned tone dispelled my inconvenient musings, and I realized three things at once. One, a tall, lanky woman had already begun emerging from one of the narrow windows, onto the roof of the lower story. Two, several men and women awaited their turn behind her. And three, the zombies around us had begun working themselves into a fury, trying to reach the tasty humans on the second floor.

Without further delay, I rolled toward the building and halted beneath the eaves. Not ten seconds later, I heard a thunk on the roof of my van. I could only assume it was the first woman I'd glimpsed, as I could no longer see the windows above me.

Over the next few minutes, I heard at least five other thunks. Unfortunately, the undead frenzy outside the van had only worsened. In fact, so many of them had pushed their way toward the smorgasbord above me that they'd begun to form a couple of piles between my van and the building, with toppled zombies forming the base and others climbing over them to reach the roof. The more zombies that approached, the higher the piles grew.

As I waited nervously in the driver's seat, I recognized the one major flaw in Operation Batshit-Crazy: I had no idea how many people I was rescuing, so I didn't know how long I needed to wait, and the zombie piles were getting bigger by the second.

I was about to signal Ray on the walkie-talkie when he beat me to the punch.

"Joe, ev'ryone on board 'cept me an' Clovis. I gotta carry him down da roof, so it's gonna take a minute. Over."

"Just hurry," I replied. "The zombies are getting closer to you. And the folks above me. Over and out."

I considered rolling down my passenger-side window and shooting some of the more ambitious creatures in the head, but before I could make a dumbass move like that, I heard whacks and gunshots from above. Clearly, those who'd landed on my roof had brought a few weapons with them, and Ray had obviously replenished their ammo from his treasure chest of a backpack.

Several zombies tumbled from the top of the surrounding piles, but the situation could still go south quickly. For those outside as well as for me and the kids.

After all, zombies were pressing against the front, back, and sides of my van, which was in imminent danger of being irreversibly encircled. Worse, I could feel the heat from the encroaching flames. Just like in the burning French Quarter.

So, when I heard the loudest thunk of all above me, I assumed Ray had finally jumped down with his human burden. My right foot shifted from the brakes and hovered over the gas pedal, but I hesitated to hit it until I was certain Ray was aboard.

Someone suddenly beat the roof of my van.

"Go. Go. Go!" Ray yelled.

I stepped on the gas and rolled forward across the grass, pushing the zombified obstacles aside and beneath me. The farther I got from the building, the faster we moved. Faster, as in going from one mile per hour to perhaps two miles per hour, but hey, at least it was progress.

Chapter

17

"I believe the most rational mind can play tricks in the dark." – Sam Daily, *The Woman in Black* (2012)

Slowly, I turned left through the zombie horde and prodded my way across the crowded parking lot. Glancing toward the burning church beside me, I noticed a creature emerge from the disintegrating foyer. Not sure what alarmed me more – that the thing wasn't on fire or that it resembled the untamed beast I'd seen on the Earhart Expressway in New Orleans.

Whatever it was, it hadn't decayed like the zombies. It was muscular and half-naked, with clawed hands and patches of coarse hair covering its body. As with the one in New Orleans, it also possessed intelligent eyes that had locked onto my face as if assessing the threat level of an obvious nemesis. As I rolled past the driveway, it remained in the burning doorway for a few more seconds, then unleashed an unholy screech and plowed through the zombies surrounding the van. It had sprinted so quickly toward me, I didn't even have a chance to warn my rooftop passengers. With ten feet left between us, it leapt upward, past my driver's-side window, and onto the top of my vehicle.

Based on the human shrieking above me, I figured the creature had nabbed someone. The zombies around us had thinned out a bit, but I still couldn't do much to shake the creature loose without shaking off all the rest of my passengers as well.

Suddenly, I saw something roll down my windshield and bounce off my hood. It was the bloody head of the first woman who'd climbed down to my van. The tall, lanky one. Her body fell off the passenger side, followed by the screeching creature. Right then, I decided I'd prefer having the chalice dent my hood again.

Some gruesome sights you just can't unsee.

Noting a temporary gap amid the teeming zombies, I prayed everyone above me had braced themselves on the roof, and then hit the gas. All of us needed to get the fuck away from the hellish situation as soon as humanly possible.

As I headed back to East Main Street, I heard multiple gunshots from above and watched several zombies fall in the glow cast from the burning church. The unseen shooters (probably Ray and at least one other person) seemed to be aiming toward the hairy, screeching creature, but it kept zigzagging through the crowd, trying to keep the undead between itself and the bullets.

Seriously, what the fuck is that thing?!

When the path ahead of me cleared enough, I flipped on my headlights and hauled ass out of the parking lot. I could hear thunks, swearing, and more gunfire above me, but I didn't stop for anything or anyone. Glancing into my newly repaired side-view mirror, I realized the creature hadn't stopped either. It was chasing us faster than any zombie could and didn't halt until I hit about thirty miles per hour. I suspected it could've caught us if it had wanted to, but instead, it just stood eerily in the empty roadway and stared at our rapidly diminishing van.

About a mile down the road, I came to a gentle stop. Then Travis and I hopped out and helped all the shaken passengers climb down from the roof, into the rear of the van. Besides Ray and Clovis, his injured friend, there were two men and three women remaining.

"We lose anyone?" I asked Ray.

"Shirley," he solemnly replied.

She must've been the tall woman the mysterious creature had unceremoniously decapitated. I'd meant anyone besides her, but I decided not to spotlight the fact that I'd driven rather recklessly from the overrun parking lot. I was just grateful the others had survived.

Once everyone had safely boarded the van, another ungodly screech echoed in the distance, as if the beast had moved on to someone else. Ray's eyes locked onto mine. His mouth was tight; his expression, grim. Or at least less stoic than usual.

We rode back to his house in near-silence. Gazing back at my passengers, I spotted Ray, Travis, Nicole, and Frankie huddled together on the floor. At my dining table, two sobbing white, middle-aged women sat across from two shell-shocked white, middle-aged men. I could only assume those were Uma, Eunice, and their husbands.

Meanwhile, an old black woman leaned against the sofa bed, cradling the injured man's head in her lap and shaking her own head with apparent dismay. Clovis grimaced and let out a mournful cry, and she responded by caressing his sweaty brow and mumbling words of reassurance.

Oh, yeah. This won't end well. For any of us.

Chapter

18

"Hey, sweetheart. Let me tell you something. You, uh, you have my permission. I ever turn into one of those things? Do me a favor, blow my fucking head off." – Steve, *Dawn of the Dead* (2004)

When we returned safely to Ray's house, he opened his garage door, and I guided my van into the available space. Fortunately, there was just enough room for me to squeeze beside the trusty pickup that had transported him and his kids from the Lake Maurepas boat launch on the fateful day the undead incursion had arrived in southern Louisiana. Once Ray had secured both of his garage doors (in case determined zombies or marauders were still in the vicinity), he and one of the other guys carried poor Clovis from the rear of my van and gently laid him on a canvas tarp on the concrete floor.

Uma and Eunice, who had met as fellow nurses in their youth, knelt on either side of their injured friend and, in the ghostly light of several electric lanterns, did their best to treat him. First, they removed the blood-soaked bandage they'd fashioned from a pink sweatshirt back in the church office. Next, they used a pair of Ray's heavy-duty scissors to cut away Clovis's jeans around the wound. Then, they tried to clean the pus-filled gash with hydrogen peroxide, which only made their patient yell in pain – and probably attract a variety of undesirables toward the only occupied house on the block.

While Ray's children took Frankie inside the kitchen to give him some overdue food and water, and the ladies' husbands disappeared into the den to allow their wives some space to work, Ray, the old black woman, and I remained in the garage. The other two no doubt stayed to lend a hand, and though I was willing to help, too – even if it meant just grabbing any necessary supplies from the house – I also attributed my presence to a certain level of morbid curiosity. As with the various times I'd slowed down on the interstate to sneak a peek at a terrible accident on the other side, I felt compelled to hover and observe the inevitable outcome.

Blood, pus, and black zombie goo seeped from the wound, which clearly resembled a deep bite. Clovis had accompanied the ladies' husbands on the first, less-successful rescue mission, and one of the rotting motherfuckers in the church had managed to take a chunk out of the poor guy's thigh.

The patient's breathing had become noticeably shallow and ragged, and his face had drained of all color, turning "a whiter shade of pale," to quote one of Clare's favorite old songs. Almost as pale as the fresh bandages Uma and Eunice utilized to wrap the wound.

Poor Clovis was still conscious, moaning periodically, with rivulets of sweat pouring from his clammy forehead. No doubt the infection had spread throughout his body, and trying to fight it had resulted in what was surely a seriously high fucking fever.

As Uma finished bandaging the wound, Eunice placed a cool rag across his brow, but we all knew it wouldn't do much good. In fact, every effort to save him was futile. If the sepsis didn't kill him first, his boiling brain surely would – and then, we'd all be in deep shit.

Ray stepped beside me. "Have ya seen dis before? Seen what happen?"

Though flattered that a badass, resourceful ex-Marine like him considered me the resident zombie expert, I still didn't know enough about the real-world, non-Hollywood undead to hazard an accurate guess. Of course, my often-reliable gut told me he (and Clovis) wouldn't like my answer.

"Well, I've certainly seen a lot of folks get bitten... hell, even torn apart... but I don't usually stick around to see what happens next." I hesitated before continuing, "Still, while I haven't actually watched someone turn into a zombie, I have seen thousands upon thousands of walking corpses... people who had been bitten or dismembered, many of whom looked recently deceased."

Although Clovis seemed too dazed to hear my words, the women had turned toward me, listening closely. I hated disappointing such kind-hearted people, but lies would only hurt them in the new fucked-up world.

"I hate to say it," I added, "but zombie bites spread the infection. And I don't think there's any way to stop it."

"He goin' into d'Infernal," the old black woman whispered, "an' one of dem dead t'ings comin' back."

I glanced at her. She was leaning against the workbench, nodding sagely. She looked familiar, but thanks to my fuzzy, fatigued brain, I couldn't figure out where, when, or how I'd seen her before, and I certainly didn't know what the hell she was talking about. Given my interest in religious history, I'd encountered a lot of different terms for the afterlife, but never the *Infernal*.

Wait a minute...

I had in fact heard that word before – earlier in the day. Miss Myriam had muttered it during my brief stay in her laundromat.

And come to think of it, the two oddballs do look a lot alike.

"Sadie, stop dat," Eunice said to the black woman, wearing the concerned yet condescending expression of a parent attempting to dissuade a child with an overactive imagination. "You know dere ain't no such place."

"Sorry, child," Sadie said with genuine sorrow. "No matter whatcha believe, Mr. Joe right... dere ain't nuttin' can be done."

Eunice's face fell, as if Sadie's words had knocked the self-assured Catholic fervor right out of her. Tears dribbled down her cheeks, and she softly sobbed.

That was all it took for Uma to start weeping, too. "Oh, Clovis," she said, sniffling.

Ray glanced at Clovis, then back at me – a silent

question in his eyes.

My chest tightened as I slowly shook my head.

For the first time since I'd met him, I saw Ray's shoulders slump in defeat.

I gazed down at Clovis and noticed he was looking up at me, his eyes wide and lucid.

Well, shit.

Apparently, he'd overheard our conversation.

His focus shifted to Ray. "I don't wanna turn into one of those godforsaken demons."

They're not demons, they're zombies. Well, except for that hairy thing. I don't know what the fuck that is.

"Ray," Clovis begged, drawing me back to the melancholy moment. "I already lost Lizabeth. It's time for me to be with her again."

A spluttering, coughing fit overtook him, and I instinctively retreated a couple of steps.

Sorry to be an asshole, buddy, but I don't want your nasty spit on me.

For all I knew, bites weren't the only way to transfer

the zombie infection.

When Clovis finally ceased coughing, he fixed his stare on Ray again. "Please, man. You need to take care of it."

Ray sighed heavily, hesitated for a few seconds, and then nodded. "OK, brother. If dat's whatcha want."

Uma and Eunice stopped sniffling and exchanged nervous glances.

"Uh, ladies," I said, "you might not want to be here for this."

Nodding sadly, they rose to their feet, said "farewell" and "Godspeed" to Clovis, and trudged into the house.

I glanced at Sadie, but she shook her head. Clearly, she wasn't going anywhere. I smiled, admiring her strength and resolve.

Then Ray knelt beside Clovis, grasped his hand, and removed a long hunting knife from his hip sheath. What a heartbreaking tableau to witness: one man suffering, the other comforting him, and both filled with peace and determination.

"Thank you, Ray," Clovis whispered before closing his eyes.

"Rest easy, Clovis," Ray replied. "Give Lizabeth my best."

Then, before he could second-guess his decision, Ray slid the knife into Clovis's head, piercing his brain through the ear canal. One sharp intake of breath, and Clovis was gone. After a few seconds, Ray withdrew the blade, wiped the blood on his friend's shirt, and replaced the knife in his hip sheath. As he rose to his feet, he kept his eyes on Clovis.

Undoubtedly, Ray had watched many fellow Marines perish. But I figured it was never easy to let your friends and loved ones go, even if you believed in a peaceful afterlife – which, sadly, I didn't. And neither did Clare.

So, unlike Clovis, I had no confidence that Clare and I would be reunited in heaven or hell. We only had one shot at happiness – in our current life, such as it was – and goddammit, she'd better be alive when I finally reached Baton Rouge. Or else, I might embark on the vigilante murder spree I'd always promised would happen in the wake of her untimely demise.

Looters and post-apocalyptic megalomaniacs, beware. If my wife is dead, your days are fucking numbered.

Chapter

19

"I can't lie to you about your chances, but... you have my sympathies." – Ash, *Alien* (1979)

Soon afterward, the shock and sadness had morphed into gratitude. Most of us, including Ray and his kids, were eager to get on the road and flee the wasteland that Gramercy had become, but we all needed a short break first.

Death-defying experiences sapped a lot of energy.

As most of us relaxed in Ray's uber-tidy den, drank some much-needed water, and tried to catch our collective breath, the two middle-aged couples (Uma and Rick, Eunice and Tony) seemed especially thankful for the successful rescue. I knew because they kept saying so – to me, Ray, the kids, even Frankie. Just as their constant *thank-you* refrain started to grate on my nerves, I changed the subject and asked them where they intended to go in the aftermath of the zombie apocalypse.

Like Ray and his two children (and now Frankie, too), they planned to venture via boat to their remote fishing camps and wait out the craziness there, however long that might take – possibly forever. Southern Louisiana boasted countless hunting and fishing havens, whether nestled along the shores of various lakes and rivers, situated on islands deep within the cypress-filled bayous, or, like the one Clare's father had owned before a nasty hurricane washed it away, balanced on pylons not far from the Gulf of Mexico. Many such camps were nothing more than cozy, raised cabins, only accessible via the water. Basically, the perfect hideouts for surviving a zombie apocalypse.

Unless, of course, zombies could swim long distances. In that case, all bets would be off. But I refrained from expressing my concerns and dampening the mood. Uma and Eunice were still upset over Shirley, their friend and fellow parishioner, who'd escaped a burning church, only to lose her head a few moments later. Of course, their other friend, Clovis, who'd accompanied their husbands in the initial rescue attempt, currently lay dead on the floor of Ray's garage, not far from my van. So, I kept my pessimistic mouth shut.

As it turned out, only Sadie intended to stay at her home in Gramercy – a fact that her church pals considered more than a little foolhardy. But really, none of us had all the answers or could predict the future, so who could attest to having the smartest plan? Maybe we were all fucked.

That said, I couldn't help but worry about my new friend – and his imminent isolation in the bayous of southern Louisiana. So, once the time had come for me to hit the road again, I tried convincing Ray to forego his fishing-camp scheme. I might've helped him rescue his cohorts, but I still felt obliged to him for saving my life and fixing my ride.

"Listen," I said when Ray and I had returned to the garage, "why don't you and your kids come with me? Frankie, too. We have a ton of space up north. We're on a lake, with lots of wooded property."

Ray smiled and shook his head. "T'anks, but we'll be safe. You can only git to our place by boat, so we don't hafta worry 'bout any of dem dead t'ings showin' up." He turned toward the workbench, scribbled something on a pad of paper, and tore off the sheet. Facing me again, he handed me the paper. "Besides, I don't do snow. Michigan too damn cold for me."

I chuckled. "I don't do snow either, believe me. But desperate times and all that…"

He smirked. "Ain't dat da trut'?"

I caught a glimpse of Clovis's covered body near the side door, and my grin faded. "Do you need some help with him? Or the bodies next door?"

"Nah, I'll take care of it. Don't wanna keep ya wife waitin' much longer."

I appreciated the fact that he didn't question whether Clare was still alive. Honestly, I had questioned it enough for the both of us.

Just then, Travis and Nicole wandered into the garage, Frankie trailing them.

Ray turned to his kids. "You two all packed up?"

"Yes, sir," Travis said.

I gazed at the paper in my hand. Ray had written down a series of GPS coordinates, along with some other numbers and the name *Cajun Corps*.

"Dat's where we'll be," he explained. "At doze coordinates."

I was touched that he trusted me with such crucial information. I assumed most military men and doomsday preppers kept those details close to their chests.

"And the rest?"

"Oh, dat's how ya can git in touch wit' us, assumin' ya got a shortwave?"

"I do, but I don't know how to use it yet," I confessed. "I'll figure it out once I get to Michigan."

Ray chuckled. "I'm sure ya will. Ya might go nuts wit'out it."

Although I needed to learn how to operate the shortwave radio I'd bought, I didn't feel the desire to explain that Clare and I would never go mad in isolation. We'd often said that, if we were the last two people on Earth, we'd be totally content. I just never realized we'd actually get the chance to prove it.

Before leaving, I took care of some overdue tasks. First and foremost, I used some toilet-tank water, hand sanitizer, dry shampoo, deodorant, and mouthwash to make myself a bit more presentable and then changed my clothes for the third time that day, wishing I'd thought to don the Home Depot poncho I'd gotten earlier before bashing and smashing more zombies.

Then, while stowing my dirty duds in the van, I made sure to remove my wallet and slip it into the back pocket of my fresh jeans (not that credit cards, money, and driver's licenses meant much anymore). I put some more water in the radiator, sprayed the van with Febreze, and hooked my phone to its charger. Last but not least, I excavated Clare's ring from the bag of dirty clothes and tucked it back inside her jewelry box – as if I'd never had to traverse a zombie-filled French Quarter to reclaim it from an overweight, over-the-hill porn king.

The less I reflect on the stupid shit I've done today, the better.

When I was finally ready, I ventured into the den and said "goodbye" and "good luck" to Uma, Eunice, Rick, and Tony. Then, Ray, Sadie, and the kids followed me into the garage for one last round of "fare-thee-wells."

Before I had a chance to say anything, Ray thrust a pair of night-vision goggles and some night-vision binoculars into my hands.

"What the hell," I said, honestly flabbergasted.

"Doze'll come in handy, believe me."

"I know, but…" I wanted to give him something in return, but he pretty much had everything he and his children needed, including a stockpile of guns, walkie-talkies, and other equipment any self-reliant, ex-military man might possess.

"No buts. Jus' take 'em." He turned to his kids. "Say bye to Mr. Joe. We flyin' da coop soon after him."

Travis reached out and shook my hand. "Good luck, Mr. Joe."

"Take care, Travis. Watch after your father and your

sister."

The boy nodded. "Yes, sir."

"Frankie, too." I glanced at the dog, who now wore a leash Travis must've swiped from the Hamiltons' house.

At the sound of his name, the dog came forward and nudged my hand. I obliged him with a vigorous head rub.

Then, without waiting for her cue, little Nicole rammed into my legs and hugged my waist. "Bye, Mr. Joe."

I leaned down and embraced her in return, the goggles and binoculars dangling from my arm. "Bye, sweetie. You be safe."

When she finally retreated, Ray extended his massive hand and shook mine firmly. "You be careful out dere," he said, his expression earnest.

"Same to you. And again, thanks for everything, Ray."

In a short amount of time, I'd made a solid friend, one I could undoubtedly trust in the future. I hoped he felt the same way about me.

"Not a problem, man. T'anks for ya help, too." He turned to Sadie, who'd remained on the steps. "Listen, couldya do me one more favor an' drop Miss Sadie off by her house? She only a li'l ways away, an' you gotta head in dat direction anyhow."

I smiled. "Sure thing."

Though eager to reach Baton Rouge, I figured I'd already delayed for less important reasons. How much harm could one more stop cause? Besides, having accomplished another near-death, adrenaline-draining experience in one long-ass day, my brain and body cried out for rest. So, maybe if I had some company, I wouldn't end up falling asleep at the wheel and crashing into a tree.

While Sadie hugged Ray, Travis, Nicole, and Frankie goodbye, I unlocked my passenger-side door, put the night-vision gear in my backpack, and shifted Azazel's carrier from the passenger seat to the floor beneath the dining table, wedging it between the table leg and one of the benches so my cat wouldn't slide around while in transit.

Ray helped Sadie into the van and pulled the door shut. Before I claimed my own seat, I crouched in front of Azazel's carrier. The damn cat had probably slept during most of the church escapade and aftermath, but at the moment, she was gazing at me with her big, sad green eyes. Feeling guilty for imprisoning her for much of the day, I opened the gate, and she promptly slunk out. A quick yoga stretch, and she hopped onto Sadie's lap. Then, from there, she jumped onto the dashboard and wedged herself against the windshield. Normally, I didn't like leaving her there while I drove, but given all the current obstacles on the road, I doubted I'd be going fast enough to endanger her.

I glanced around the van to ensure everything was secure, then slid behind the wheel, clicked my seatbelt in place, and gave Ray the thumbs-up signal. He gazed toward the side door, where Travis was presumably keeping watch for zombies or other dangers in the driveway. Then he grinned at me, pressed the button to open the garage door, and waved goodbye.

Waving in return, I reversed the van down the driveway, backed onto the street, and headed off with my latest passenger.

Chapter

20

"You know nothing. Hell is only a word. The reality is much, much worse." – Dr. Weir, *Event Horizon* (1997)

After a few darkened blocks, I turned to my passenger. "Where to, Miss Sadie?"

"Keep goin' down dis road 'til it turn to dirt," she

replied. "Den take da first right."

She reached across the dashboard and stroked Azazel. The fact that my tiny tiger allowed an unfamiliar woman to touch her astonished me. Normally, she wasn't very friendly to anyone but me and Clare, and yet there she lay, stretched out on the dash, getting her leopard-spotted belly rubbed by a complete stranger.

Sadie must've felt my stare. She pivoted toward me and winked. "Got a sense aroun' animals," she explained. "I like dem an' dey like me."

"That's a useful gift to have," I said, turning back to the windshield just in time to clip a sprinting zombie and propel it onto a random front lawn.

"Nah, I barely got any," she lamented. "My sister got all da real gifts."

A sister? So, I was right. No wonder Sadie had seemed so familiar. I knew exactly where I'd seen her before – or, rather, where I'd seen her likeness. She had the same round figure, the same jovial grin, and the same penetrating brown eyes. She was just a slightly older version.

"You don't, by any chance, have a sister named Myriam Beauvoir?"

A huge smile spread across her face. "Ya know Myriam?"

"Sure do," I said. "I lived in the Quarter for a long time. Used to do my laundry at her place."

A wave of sadness crashed over me. I'd said I *lived* in the Quarter. Hard to believe I'd only left my home that morning. Shit, a lot had happened since then.

"Anyway," I continued, "we were friends..." I almost laughed at what I'd said, considering how Myriam had always felt about me. "Well, actually, my wife was friends with her."

In the glow of my headlights, I spotted a small cluster of zombies traipsing down the steps of a large double shotgun house, sporting a slew of gaping wounds and other disgusting features. One of the undead creatures was even chowing on a severed hand.

Yet another image I can't unsee.

As a few of the zombies stepped into the road, I swerved to the right and knocked two of them into the others, sending them all tumbling down like rotten bowling pins.

"You should know," I added, "your sister is still alive. At least she was when I left New Orleans this morning."

She grinned again. "No way deez creatures ever git Myriam." Spoken with absolutely no doubt.

I couldn't bring myself to mention that the spreading fires were more likely to kill her long before the zombies would.

"Yeah, Myriam knows how to handle herself." I turned to Sadie. "You ladies seem to know more about these monsters than the rest of us. Care to fill me in?"

"Darlin', doncha know? Deez da end of days," she said solemnly. "D'Infernal done open up an' release its badness into da world."

"You mean, when there's no more room in hell..." I started to quip, but then immediately stopped talking at the sight of a four-hundred-pound zombie cook, still dressed in his work duds.

Quickly, I swerved to the left to avoid him. My zombie-mobile was sturdy, but I feared hitting something with that much heft could do some real damage – or at least slap another foul-smelling coat of goop on my baby.

"Nah, deez creatures... leas' some of 'em... come t'ru da veil."

I didn't have a ready response, but she must've noticed my quizzical look because she continued her bizarre explanation.

"Look, child," she said patiently, as if explaining a basic concept to a simpleton, "dis world we live in, it ain't da only place. Dere many udders."

I took a measured breath. Although I'd always enjoyed reading books (or, more often, watching documentaries) about religious histories and conspiracies, I'd never believed in anything beyond reality.

But who am I to judge Sadie's beliefs – or her sister's?
Fucking zombies are walking the planet.

"So," I asked, straining to comprehend, "the veil, as you call it, separates different dimensions. And the Infernal is one of them? Is it like another Earth?"

She pursed her lips, as if trying to form the simplest answer. "Guess ya could say da Infernal is anudder version of here. Where we go when we pass."

I squinted in confusion. "So, it's like hell?"

She shook her head. "No. No place like dat. Dere normal people in da Infernal... but dere also monsters."

My brow furrowed even more.

"It jus' anudder place we go, but when we get dere, not all of us is good. Some turn bad. Real bad." She sighed. "Seems some of da bad ones found dere way back here an' cause dis mess. Don't t'ink dey can git back."

If I understood Sadie correctly, she'd basically told me that a separate dimension existed from our own. Likely just another facet of the multiverse – a theory that many scientists had long embraced.

Supposedly, that adjacent dimension – a place she and her sister called the Infernal – contained evil beings, essentially zombies, that had busted a hole in the universe and entered our world.

Either the stupid I-World Initiative had caused the breach, or else, it was just a coincidence that poor Dibya had detected it when she did.

That crazy-ass theory might explain the zombies – sort of – but what about those hairy creatures? Like the one that had shredded the six assholes planning to carjack me? Or the one that had freaked my shit out back at the church in Gramercy?

"Zombies aren't the only things that came through, right?"

She shook her head again. "Dere's monsters way worse."

"I don't know if you saw it back at the church, but there's something else. Something way smarter than the zombies, but with a wild look in its eyes. Plus tufts of hair, big teeth, and nasty-looking claws. Sort of like a werewolf, for lack of a better term."

She nodded vehemently. "Oh, yeah, I saw it. Dey call 'em wildlings on d'udder side. But over here, we call it da rougarou. It's a mad beast. Crazy. Violent. Ya stay clear of dem, or dey bite cha fool head off."

Shit, woman, you don't have to tell me twice.

I scanned the trees lining the road, suddenly worried the "rougarou" had followed us from the church. "I'll definitely keep that in mind."

"Turn here," Sadie abruptly said.

Slowing down to comply with her instructions, I realized I hadn't even noticed we'd been bumping along a dirt road for a while, so engrossed had I been in our conversation. Still, the last-minute errand had taken way longer than Ray had suggested it would, when he'd asked me to drive Sadie home. Maybe he didn't think it really mattered how long it took me to reach Baton Rouge. Perhaps he didn't believe I had much of a chance of ever seeing my wife alive again.

Shaking loose the negative thoughts, I focused instead on the road ahead. It narrowed considerably and eventually turned into a single lane. Fewer undead creatures meandered around the wooded area than back in downtown Gramercy, but I still spotted a few here and there. After winding my way along the curvy dirt road and rumbling over several small bridges, I was about to ask Sadie how much longer the drive might take when the road suddenly dead-ended at a modest house, surrounded by a grove of pecan trees.

"Dis da place," Sadie announced.

I'd figured as much – and unfortunately, several zombies milled about on her driveway. They hadn't reached her house yet, but they perked up when my headlight beams hit them.

"Shit," I said.

I came to a halt several yards from the zombies, unbuckled my seatbelt, and headed to the sofa bed. Hoping to conserve my shotgun shells for more immediate dangers, I opened the hidden storage compartment and removed my AR-15. Besides, I figured a bit more practice with the rifle couldn't hurt.

A moment later, I heard an exasperated sigh from the passenger seat. "Whatcha doin', boy? My sugar can take care of 'em."

Once again, I had no idea what the hell Sadie was talking about – and had little time to waste – so I opened one of the rear doors, hopped onto the gravel driveway, and knelt on the ground to take aim.

The first two zombies (appropriately dressed in jeans and work shirts, given the rustic environment) hit the ground after four shots. Using two bullets to drop each of them wasn't terrible, considering how exhausted I was, but the third zombie posed a problem. He wore an expensive, black-leather motorcycle outfit and sported a shaded helmet, and while the bullets could technically penetrate the fiberglass, the biker still hadn't fallen after three shots.

"Dat's da idiot who bin rentin' d'ol' Smitty place down da road," I heard Sadie shout from the front of the van. "He race fancy motorbikes."

"Great," I mumbled as I took aim once more.

Before I could pull the trigger, though, I heard the passenger door slide open and watched Sadie step down onto the driveway, directly into my line of sight.

As soon as her shoes touched the gravel, she shut the door and started screaming at the top of her lungs, "Sugar! Sugar! Come an' git it!"

Then she scurried toward me (much faster than I would've expected, given her size), yanked me to my feet, and tugged me toward the rear of my van. After she clambered aboard, I followed suit and closed the door. As I trailed her to the front seats and opened my mouth to ask what the hell was happening, I spotted a fourteen-foot alligator sauntering across the headlight beams. Then, without hesitation, the giant creature latched onto the zombie's ankle and yanked it to the ground. A scary and thrilling sight to behold.

"You have a pet gator?"

"Sugar no one's pet. He jus' live here."

Shit, she wasn't kidding. Animals really do like her.

The gator didn't simply destroy the zombie; he bit its helmeted head clean off and spit it into the nearby marsh. I only hoped that chomping on zombies wouldn't someday turn Sugar into a carnivorous, undead alligator. What a nightmarish creature that would be!

Sadie opened the passenger-side door again and stepped down from the van.

Instinctively, I scooped up Azazel from the dashboard, in case she had a sudden desire to hop through the open doorway and introduce herself to Sugar – or, more likely, hiss at the gator and lose her own furry head in the marsh.

Clutching my disgruntled cat against my chest, I looked down at Sadie. "Sure you're gonna be alright?"

She beamed. "Might not got Myriam's gifts, but I know how to keep da dead away."

I glanced through the windshield, and sure enough, my headlights had illuminated several rosemary bushes lining her front porch. They had obviously prevented the zombies from getting too close to the house.

Man, I wonder if rosemary would grow in northern Michigan. Could it survive the harsh winters?

"T'anks for da lift," she said, waving goodbye. "Good luck to you an' yours."

"Same to you."

I slid the door closed, but Sadie only took a few steps before I spotted two separate clusters of zombies heading her way. Sugar couldn't possibly dispatch all of them before they reached her, and unfortunately, Sadie was already halfway between the van and her house. Though feisty for her age, I knew she couldn't make it to safety in time.

With a heavy sigh, I set Azazel on her carrier. "Be good, tiny tiger." Then I picked up the rifle. "I'll be back in a minute."

She squinted at me, as if tired of hearing me say that – and watching me go. Maybe she worried about my safety – or, more likely, hated being left behind.

Either way, I didn't have time to placate her. Instead, I hopped to the ground, secured the door, and rushed toward Sadie.

Her head pivoted from side to side, and her waddling gait sped up. Apparently, she'd noticed the converging zombies – but not soon enough.

As I neared her, I fired my rifle at the closest creatures on the left and right. Finding it hard to aim while running, I made no kill shots, but I slowed them down just enough to scoop the old woman up and carry her toward the house. She was no lightweight, but pure adrenaline propelled me forward, and we reached her porch just in time.

While she hastened to unlock her door, I stood guard, striving to keep the monsters at bay. But the rosemary bushes did the job for me. Just like the plants in front of Myriam's laundromat, Sadie's prevented the zombies from climbing the porch.

Unhappily, though, more and more creatures emerged from the surrounding swamp. By the time Sadie opened the door and ushered me inside, perhaps forty undead creatures had converged on her front lawn.

Wearing a fretful expression, she peered out the nearest window. "Shoot, child. Don't know where all deez comin' from."

I stood beside her, trying to catch my breath.

She turned to me. "T'anks for dat, boy. 'Preciate da help."

"You're welcome," I replied. "But I seem to have a problem. It's a long walk back to my van."

"Yeah, ya right. Dat's a lot of dead t'ings in my front yard, an' dey jus' keep comin'." She sighed. "Dere's a bottlin' plant down da road. Wonder if dat's where dey came from?"

Thanks to the moonlight, I could see that most of the zombies outside wore matching uniforms. Gray overalls, splashed with blood and black goo. Some had open wounds. Some were missing limbs or chunks of flesh. Some sported all of the above.

You know, the usual.

"Makes sense." I watched as the horde continued to grow. "Exactly how many people are typically on a shift at the bottling plant?"

"How should I know? Maybe two hund'ed?"

I gazed at the undulating mass of undead. "Yep, seems

about right."

My rifle had maybe ten rounds left, so I certainly couldn't shoot my way out.

I scanned the trees, noting even more zombies headed our way. "Why are they all gathering here? Shouldn't some of them be heading to your neighbors?"

"Don't got many," she replied, "an' da ones I do have prob'ly dead by now."

"So, we're the only food nearby?"

"'Fraid so."

"Well, shit."

Sugar sauntered across the yard, tearing through the zombies, but after a few minutes, the horde swarmed her, and she vanished from our view.

"She be OK," Sadie assured me. "No way dey turn her over, an' her top skin too tough for dem to bite t'ru."

Well, sadly, I didn't possess a hide as impenetrable as the alligator's. And neither did Azazel.

Beyond the zombified mosh pit, I could see her through the windshield. She'd hopped onto the dashboard – searching for her daddy perhaps or just curious about all the moaning outside the van. Several zombies had spotted her and turned in her direction, but luckily, I'd locked all the doors – and the windows were fortified.

She was likely safer than I was. Too bad I'd never taught her how to drive.

*Who am I kidding? She'd probably throw it in
reverse and leave her dumbass daddy behind.*

Desperate to return to my cat, I asked, "Is there a way
out the back?"

Sadie shook her head mournfully. "Da house back up
to da bayou. Too deep to walk, so ya gotta swim. Den
anudder gator might getcha. Dey active 'bout now."

"Zombies to the left of me," I murmured. "Gators to
the right. Here I am, stuck in the middle with you."

She flashed me a puzzled look. "Whatcha say?"

"Nothing." I sighed. "Just remembering an old song."

Recognition dawned in her eyes. "Oh, yeah, I 'member
dat one." She hummed a verse.

"Look, Sadie, I gotta get outta here. Clare's waitin' for
me."

My tone bordered on whiny, but I didn't care.

With a nod, she abruptly stopped humming and
waddled toward the rear of the small house. I followed her to
a sliding glass door, through which I spied a narrow porch,
lined with rosemary plants, and a bayou less than twenty feet
away. A rickety dock led into the moonlit water, and a flat-
bottomed Cajun pirogue floated beside the pylons.

A dream fishing camp – if not surrounded by zombies.

"I could ring da suppa bell," Sadie suggested, pointing

to a nearby pecan tree, where two ropes hung from a low branch – one bound to a metal tire rim and the other tied to a giant bolt. "Used to be how I called my boys home for suppa."

She wore a wistful expression, as if remembering happier days – back when her family lived with her and she regularly cooked for them. Probably a giant pot of gumbo or jambalaya.

I longed to ask Sadie where her children had gone – and if they were even still alive – but it didn't seem like the most ideal time for a heart to heart.

"Well," I said, "I don't know if it'll be enough to lure the zombies back here, but it's the only plan we've got." I turned to Sadie. "I can ring it until most of the zombies reach the sides of the house. Hopefully, that'll clear the front yard a bit, enough for me to run through your place and out the front door." My brow furrowed. "But will you be OK after I go?"

She smiled warmly. "Don't worry 'bout me, child. Da rosemary'll hold 'em back." She winked. "An' I gotta few udder tricks up my sleeve."

"Alright then. If you're sure..."

"I'm sure. Like ya said, ya wife waitin' for ya."

Quietly, we slid the door open, and leaving my rifle behind, I ventured toward the supper bell. I tried to walk as carefully as possible, but the wooden porch and weathered steps creaked nonetheless. Not that it mattered – the collective moaning out front likely drowned out my footsteps.

Once I reached the tree, I grabbed the dangling bolt and turned around. Sadie gave me a thumbs-up, and with a deep breath, I started banging on the rim – which made an ungodly racket.

No wonder it had worked as a supper bell. The clanging sounds likely drifted far across the bayous, where her husband and kids once fished, telling them to come home for the night.

Only, I wasn't looking out at the water. I was watching the perimeter of Sadie's house. After a minute or so of constant clanging, several zombies appeared on either side, avoiding the rosemary plants and trudging toward me. When at least a hundred walking corpses seemed to be headed my way, and the pathway back to the house had shrunk to a perilous width, I figured the time had come to make a break for it.

But just then, Sadie hollered, "Da boys are comin'!"

"What?" I yelled, still whacking the rim with the bolt.

She pointed toward the water behind me. For a split second, I assumed her husband and sons were headed home, but when I whirled around, I spotted at least a dozen lengthy gators swimming toward the shore.

"Holy crap!"

Most people likely believed that gators were only fast in the water, but they'd be dead wrong. The damn things could display bursts of speed exceeding thirty miles per hour. And as surprising as this revelation might seem... I, myself, couldn't run thirty miles an hour. Not even the fastest human on the planet could – and I was pretty fucking far from the fastest.

"Come on, you gotta be kidding!" I dropped the bolt and sprinted toward the back porch.

Glancing back, I realized the gators had picked up speed – and I was definitely their primary target. Of course, my rapid movement had also animated the damn zombies, so they, too, had quickened their pace.

Two of the gators outran the others. I could hear them snapping at my heels. Meanwhile, the zombified plant workers closed in from the edges, and Sadie stood directly in the door opening, wearing a shell-shocked expression.

"Outta the way!" I hollered.

Both gators converged just as several moaning zombies stumbled onto the path behind me. But I didn't take the time to look back. I just leapt up the steps and bolted through the doorway, tripping over my own feet and landing hard on the wooden floor.

A few seconds later, Sadie had closed and locked the glass door.

"You OK, boy?"

I exhaled and staggered to my feet. "I'm good. Just wish I'd realized the supper bell wasn't only intended for humans."

She grinned sheepishly. "Sorry. Didn' t'ink so many would come."

Beyond the glass, it looked as though the gators had turned on the zombies – and foolishly, the zombies were trying to bite the gators. My money was on the reptiles.

With no time to waste, I grabbed my gun and headed for the front door. Stepping onto the porch, I spotted several zombies in the front yard, but not as many as before – and only a few near the van, ogling Azazel.

I turned to Sadie, who'd followed me to the door. "Maybe you should come with me."

"Nah, dis my home."

"That's exactly what your sister said."

She smiled. "We alike in a lotta ways."

"True dat."

"Be careful out dere on da road."

"I'll try," I replied. "You take care, too."

"Oh, don't worry 'bout me," she said, sounding as stubborn as her sister. "I'll be jus' fine."

"I'm sure you will."

Then, with a chuckle, I stepped off the porch and darted toward the van. About halfway there, I suddenly remembered Sugar. Though the zombies had dispersed, I didn't see her anywhere.

Jesus, did they eat her?

Of course, I should've known better. Turning back, I noticed her lying on Sadie's porch. Her tail hung down the steps, as if she'd just sauntered up there. The old woman knelt beside her, patting her head and handing her a chunk of fresh meat.

I shook my head and edged toward the van. Four zombies stood around the front, grabbing at the barred windows and fixated on Azazel. Although she'd locked eyes with mine, the walking corpses had yet to notice me. So, I lifted my gun and shot all four of them. Oddly enough, they were much easier to kill when I was standing in one place, being ignored.

Quickly, I unlocked the driver's-side door and slipped inside the van. Gazing back at the house, I noticed Sadie standing in her front entrance. She waved once and then shut the door, leaving the giant alligator guarding her porch. No wonder she'd be just fine.

What a strange fucking world it's become.

I stowed the AR-15, checked all the doors, and again secured the cat carrier on the front passenger seat, if only to make it easier for me to coax Azazel back inside somewhere down the road. Depending on what was happening at my mother-in-law's house, I might not have a chance to wrangle her then. After reclaiming my own seat, I reversed down the driveway, turned my van around, and retraced the route back to a road I recognized.

Leaning over to rub Azazel's chin, I whispered, "Next stop: Grandma's house. This time, I swear it."

Fifteen minutes after leaving Sadie's little cabin in the woods, I'd found my way back to Airline Highway. I couldn't believe it had taken me all goddamn day to go such a short distance. Obviously, I was way behind in my trek to reach Clare, and I was fucking determined not to get sidetracked again.

Sidetrack. That's Clare's nickname. Not mine, dammit.

I sighed. The longer we stayed apart, the more likely we'd never be together again. And there was no fucking way I'd let that happen.

Glancing at the dashboard, I noticed Azazel had fallen asleep again. Normally, I wouldn't have wanted her to be curled up on the dash while in transit, but thanks to the stalled vehicles, occasional traffic, and meandering zombies everywhere, I was driving slowly enough to avoid the possibility of her smacking her head on the glass or rolling onto the floor.

Heading north on U.S. 61 and doing my best to stay alert and avoid any life-threatening obstacles, I found my thoughts wandering back to Sadie and wondering if, like her sister, she was also a voodoo priestess. As focused as I was on reaching Clare as soon as possible, a part of me wished I'd taken the time to ask Sadie some more questions about what had happened to cause the global nightmare. Even after our brief conversation, I was no closer to understanding what had created the fucktard situation in the first place.

When Clare and I had listened to Samir's bizarre warning and discussed its unbelievable ramifications, we'd understood that the trouble all began with an intercepted signal of some kind. Perhaps a message from a foreign power that inexplicably wanted to end the world or maybe some kind of bullshit alien conspiracy.

Sadie, on the other hand, believed the creatures had come from some alternate dimension. Actually, she and her sister had called it the Infernal, whatever that was, and implied that a breach between dimensions had opened up, releasing these fucked-up things into our world.

Even given my lifelong love of horror and sci-fi and weirdness in general, the whole situation still seemed crazy, unlikely, and frankly impossible. But holy shit, it was really happening, wasn't it? I might've smacked my head a couple times that morning, but I hadn't dreamed the entire day. Or had I?

No. This all feels and smells too fucking real to be merely a concussion-fueled nightmare.

The sad truth was that I wouldn't get any answers – not anytime soon. For the moment, all that mattered, all that made sense, was to continue down the highway, keeping my windshield pointed toward the state capital, aiming for Clare, and hoping for safety. And maybe, down the road, even a bit of serenity.

It felt like Azazel and I had a long fucking way to go before we could collect her mama and make it up to northern Michigan, but goddammit, we were gonna get there.

Chapter

21

"Ninety-seven percent of nationwide coverage, and we get stuck in the three percent." – Doug Bukowski, *The Hills Have Eyes* (2006)

Ten minutes passed, and we'd traveled farther than we had in the first hour of our never-ending journey from New Orleans to Baton Rouge. The highway to hell had gone rural, and the auto traffic and ambling zombies had cleared out quite a bit.

In fact, without my constant need to alternate between the brakes and the gas, the ride had smoothed out considerably. So much so that Azazel felt comfortable enough to stretch her legs and jump down from the dash.

That was when everything changed. Again.

As Azazel leapt downward, her tail caught my cellphone, knocking it onto the floor. Naturally, the resulting thunk freaked her out, and she darted toward the back of the van – surely to find a safe hiding place from the startling sound she herself had just created.

Shaking my head in amusement, I leaned down and picked up the phone to reconnect it to the charger. Suddenly, I noticed the light blinking above my screen. With my eyes on the dimly lit road, I lifted the phone and unlocked the home screen.

I had a text notification. A motherfucking text!

My hands trembled as I brought up the messaging app with one hand and kept the other on the steering wheel.

It was from Clare. She was alive. My baby was fucking alive!

Fuck everyone who doubted it. Including me.

I slowed the van, opened the message, and scanned

the text quickly.

Joe, I hope you can read this. I was so happy when I got your text. I thought something terrible had happened. Where are you? Mom and I are in trouble. The house is surrounded. Must be a few hundred out there, if not more. They know we're in here, and they're trying to get to us. Not sure how long we can hold out. Please hurry. I love you.

"Fuck. Fuck. FUCK!"

It looked as though she'd sent the text about an hour before, but my phone hadn't received it until that moment.

Goddammit. All my fucking screwing around.

Maybe I'd helped some people in need, but in doing so, I'd left the love of my life vulnerable. She was in trouble – deep shit, no less – and I was still out and about, doing all kinds of stupid crap, everything but making a beeline for her. Clare had always been the most important person in the world to me, and I refused to fucking fail her.

I immediately braked the van and tried dialing her number. But I didn't even get the bullshit *all-circuits-are-busy* voice. There was zero signal. Not one damn bar.

Not only had the zombie apocalypse disrupted America's communications networks, but since I was driving through the middle of bumfuck nowhere, there probably wasn't even a cell tower anywhere near me.

I heard a meow from behind me. Glancing over my shoulder, I caught a glimpse of Azazel slinking toward the front of the van. Her eyes met mine, and she paused below the passenger seat. I must've forgotten to latch the gate when securing her carrier, so it had opened during the ride, and as it swung toward me, she reached her paws upward and scrambled inside.

She'd always been a smart cat, and she could usually read my moods well. Anger made her bolt from the room, but fear and sickness often brought her closer.

In the present case, she likely knew that something serious had occurred. She'd heard the panic in my voice, and no matter what I was about to do to get back to her beloved mama, she apparently felt a lot more at ease inside her carrier. Grinning, I leaned over and secured the gate.

Knowing Azazel was relatively safe, I slammed my foot onto the gas pedal, and the van careened down the highway. The next several minutes passed in a veritable blur as I bulldozed my way toward Baton Rouge. I didn't recall much of what occurred. Whenever a stalled vehicle or stumbling zombie appeared in my path, I didn't even swerve my van. Just rammed into it and not-so-politely shoved it aside with the welded steel bars above my front bumper.

Cuz fuck them.

Azazel let out a tiny *don't-let-any-fuckers-stop-us* meow.

If anything or anyone got in my way, he, she, or it would soon be out of my way. Clare was counting on me – and, for that matter, so was my cat.

Survive the Zombie Chaos

CONTINUE THE CHAOS

Terror on the Bayou: Zombie Chaos Book 3

**Many things can kill you on the bayou...
gators, snakes, crazy Cajuns, and now zombies.**

I'm another step closer to reaching my wife, Clare. But you know the old saying... one step forward, two steps back. The problem is time... as in, it's running out. For her. And for us.

Not to mention, Azazel is upset that she's still not with her mama. Flesh-eating zombies are bad enough, but soon, I'm gonna have one pissed-off kitty on my hands, and that's never a good thing.

Terror on the Bayou is the third book in the ***Zombie Chaos*** series, a post-apocalyptic tale filled with graphic language, graphic gore, and, naturally, graphic snark.

Continue the chaos with ***Terror on the Bayou: Zombie Chaos Book 3***

https://www.amazon.com/dp/B084T43GMB

Get a FREE short story from the point of view of Joe's cat, Azazel, as she embarks on her own zombie-killing adventure... yep, you heard that right. She's thirteen pounds of zombie-killing fury. Follow the link to receive your free copy of **Azazel the Zombie Slayer**. All we ask is that you sign up for our newsletter.

FREE SHORT STORY –
https://BookHip.com/CJNLNS

Even if you don't want the short, you can still join our newsletter.

Stay alive and join us by becoming a Survivor (http://zombiechaos.com/become-a-survivor).

We know you love your freedom, so we promise not to bombard you with junk mail. We'll only notify you about new releases, giveaways, and recommendations.

If you enjoyed **Highway to Hell: Zombie Chaos Book 2**, please consider leaving a positive review.

About the Authors

D.L. Martone is the joint pen name of husband-wife duo Daniel and Laura Martone. Part-time residents of New Orleans and northern Michigan, the Martones travel the country in their mobile writing studio, a cozy RV dubbed *Serenity*. As you might have guessed, they're huge fans of *Firefly*, which is why they remodeled the interior of their travel trailer to resemble Captain Reynolds' beloved spaceship. Together, they enjoy writing space opera, LitRPG GameLit, urban fantasy, cozy mysteries, and, of course, post-apocalyptic zombie tales.

Acknowledgments

We appreciate the support from our friends, family, and fellow writers – and the inspiration gleaned from various zombie flicks and TV shows, especially *Shaun of the Dead*, *The Walking Dead*, and George Romero's *Dead* movies – as well as our fellow fans of such stories.

Of course, we couldn't have continued this series (or finished this book) without the love and support of each other and our beloved kitty, Ruby Azazel.

Lastly, we're grateful to you, our fellow survivors, for joining Joe on his harrowing journey through zombie-filled Louisiana.

www.ingramcontent.com/pod-product-compliance
Lightning Source LLC
Chambersburg PA
CBHW050517260626
47157CB00004B/1365